WAITING FOR GILBERT

HOLIDAYS IN HADLEY SPRINGS
BOOK ONE

TASHA HACKETT

To receive email updates about future works, sales, devotionals, and deleted scenes, request to join Tasha's newsletter by emailing tashahackett.author@gmail.com

©2024 by Tasha Hackett.

Edited by Megan Schaulis and Crystal Nielson

Cover graphics from Canva.

Paperback ISBN: 978-1-965778-01-2

Ebook ISBN: 978-1-965778-00-5

Tasha's mission is to produce content that positively reinforces Christian values. Her novels depict achievable relationships between flawed characters loved by an unflawed God.

Praise for *Waiting for Gilbert*

"What a fun read! The banter is delightful and clever. The book is intimate and sexy while still staying clean. The Christian message touched my heart and made me tear up. I highly recommend this book!" —Victorine E. Lieske, *New York Times* and *USA Today* bestselling author

"A fun, sweet, touching Christmas tale that I thoroughly enjoyed. It is going to be on my re-read shelf." —Mary Connealy, award-winning author of more than 75 historical comedies with cowboys

"Tasha Hackett proves she's every bit as adept with contemporary romance as historical in this snowy sweet tale. With a lovably unique heroine and a steadfast, cello-playing hero, *Waiting for Gilbert* is grab-your-favorite-cozy-blanket perfection!" — Megan Schaulis, author of *The Susa Chronicles*

"Full of laugh out loud humor. An adorable romance, and quirky but lovable characters that could walk off the page, *Waiting for Gilbert* is the perfect cozy read for anyone who loves love!" —Emily Barnett, author of *Thread of Dreams*

"I adore this story. With genuine and honest characters that leap off the page, *Waiting for Gilbert* is small town romance with heart. Perfect for fans of rom-com and Christian romance." —Tosca Lee, *New York Times* bestselling author and three-time International Book Award winner

For Michelle, who will forever be a big sister
&
For my bosom friend, Heather—a kindred spirit

"Well, one can't get over the habit of
being a little girl all at once."
—L.M. Montgomery, *Anne of Green Gables*

CORDELIA

THURSDAY, DECEMBER 14

ELVIS PRESLEY—BLUE CHRISTMAS

Squinting at the blowing snow through my windshield while sad and pathetic breakup tears drip down my snotty face isn't how I pictured my day going. I was going to be *strong*. I was going to be the strongest, toughest woman you'd ever seen. *Psh!* Shaun? Who's he? Me? Engaged? Nope. It was like it never happened. A fling! A little run-o-the-mill date'em and drop'em. That's how I roll. I'm made of steel, and I'm bad and tough and do what I want.

I make a popping noise with my lips—the one that drove my sister crazy when I was a kid. The hum of the engine and the warm air blasting through the vents are the only other sounds in the car as I tell these lies to myself in a hopeless attempt to stall another round of tears.

Let it be known that strong women cry. Sometimes a lot. But only because being alone is the worst. Not because I wanted to spend the rest of my life with Shaun.

You know what? I'm glad Shaun called off the wedding. Someone needed to wake us up. I just wish I had thought of it first. We hadn't even sent the save-the-dates. See? Let's be thankful for that little blessing.

Breakups are yucky and sad even when it's best to get out of a relationship that isn't working. I know this.

I knew something was off between us. He was nice. But man, were we boring together.

I release a shuddering breath and veer left off of Highway Eighty-One. My next turn is nearby and I don't want to miss it again, so I pull over onto the shoulder. I fish another tissue from my purse and blow my nose throughout another pep talk. "Shaun did the right thing." *Sniffle.* "Shaun is not the bad guy." *Hiccup.* "I am not the bad guy." *Blow.* "It hurts now, but it will be better soon."

Last week, after a *meh* sort of date, he'd ducked his head once and then looked me straight in the eyes to deliver his breakup lines. "Cordy, you're cute and fun, but I don't see us having a family together. The longer we're engaged, it just doesn't feel right anymore. I know there's someone perfect for you and it's not me. It's been a great two years." With soul-wrenching pity in his eyes he shrugged because there was nothing else to say.

The message is loud and clear. I'm not the kind of person men want to have families with.

Was it because the music was too loud at dinner and I *could not* stop bobbing my head and dipping my shoulders? The dance-party-for-one embarrassed him? Or maybe when I created an entire backstory for our server's tattoo of an apple on her forearm. I'd concluded she was only waiting tables to save for tuition to transfer to Oxford and learn from the great scholars in England and her apple was a symbol of knowledge to propel her toward her quest. When I asked her—Shaun absolutely hated that I asked because it was "none of our business," but I figure if you get a big ol' tattoo on your arm, maybe you want to talk about it?—she giggled and raised her arm saying, "I just looove Edward Cullen, yeah?"

"Oooh." I blinked. "Me too!"

Shaun sighed because he knew I was lying. So I kept talking to spite him. "Me too. *Mmhmmm*. It's *crazy* what some people say about Edward being controlling and abusive."

Her jaw dropped. "I'm bringing you a free dessert."

Yeah. It's wrong to lie. If I'd known she was going to go nuts on me about it and act like we were new besties, I wouldn't have said it. Ugghhh. No. Shaun didn't dump me because of one boring date.

But he's right. I'm twenty-eight years old. Maybe it's time for a change. Maybe there's a reason. A real, good solid reason that I'm not the kind of person men want to be with.

Fine, then! I vow not to be cute and fun. It's my Christmas promise to myself. I shall not be cute. I shall not be fun.

Who's Cordelia Jane? Not me. I have a serious name henceforth. I'm known across the country as plain CJ. I'm *serious* and I'm *focused*. And *dang it*, I'm crying again.

I dig in the door pocket for a handful of brown paper napkins leftover from lunch.

Settling for Shaun was a mistake. He was never my Gilbert. I know this now.

My mom is obsessed with *Anne of Green Gables*. Hence my sister's name, Diana, and my name, Cordelia. Who names their daughter Cordelia??? My mom. From one little conversation in the book when Anne says to Marilla, "I would love to be called Cordelia. It's such a perfectly elegant name."

Sure it is. But elegant names do not beget elegant futures.

Regardless, I grew up watching Jonathon Crombie as Gilbert Blythe patiently woo Anne Shirley, and I childishly built the same fantasy for myself. I decided to wait for that. I would wait for my Gilbert. Since my hair is as bright red as Anne's, I've always identified with her on a personal level.

When did I lose that dream? I scoff at the foolishness of it. The perfect man isn't going to come knocking on my door in the middle of the night. I must go find him!

I can't sit here and wait for some dashing, pre-med student from Canada to find me. I must take direct action. I'll create an online dating profile. Yes! Then I'll have the means to sift through potential candidates before I get caught in their sweet faces and adoring smiles.

Despite his good looks, Shaun was not Gilbert. Besides our limited passion—maybe because of—we never fought. He just gave me a disappointed look on occasion. Shaun doesn't even like to read!

I smack my forehead on the steering wheel.

How did I ever think it would work between us?

Currently I'm trying to get to my sister's house in tiny Hadley Springs, Nebraska. Not because I'm running away. That's something a cute and fun girl might do. No, I'm a serious, focused career girl looking for a house to rent, and I'm not too proud to live with my sister and all of her adorable gremlins until I find the perfect place. Also, Christmas.

My phone's light momentarily blinds me when I check the map. At five thirty it's already as dark as midnight here in the Midwest.

Okay, I'm going the right direction. I shut off the screen because I'm not the kind of girl who needs a phone to tell her where to go every second. And because I've been here five times and I should know this already. I pull back onto the deserted road just as my phone buzzes with an incoming call from my cousin. I tap my earbud to answer. "Mark Brader! The one and only!"

"Hey, Cordy."

I smile. My favorite cousin, editor, and friend also happens to be an odd sort of coach who doesn't take crap from me ever. Not since our days at college and not since we both started working in the publishing world. He with the editing. Me with the writing—and the cooking and picture-taking as a food photographer. He spends his days making authors cry from an office in Phoenix, and I do cookbooks. It's my job to test recipes and write lovely blurbs to convince people to cook the food. That's my jam. Sometimes literally. I did a whole book on different jams once.

"Mark! Where you been all my life?" We talked yesterday.

He takes a noisy sip of his coffee. I know it's coffee because if there wasn't a cup nearby he'd have it through an IV into his bloodstream. I imagine a no-nonsense black mug with his alma mater in a gold scrolling logo that he carefully clicks into place on a little mug heater. He would have one of those because he's too uppity to put it in a thermos like the rest of us peasants. Mark would probably explain that coffee tastes better when given the chance to aerate.

"What's up?" I sniff from the leftover Shaun emotions, and I'm instantly regretting the action. *Nooo.* But it's too late.

"Uh-oh. You sick?"

"Nope," I squeak.

"Shaun." He spits the name like an expletive.

"Don't distract me. I am *serious* and *focused.*"

"And I'm a dancing monkey."

"Good. So we needn't argue. Take note, I'm changing my name to CJ."

"Oh, we are serious," he says.

"And focused."

"So... CJ, hit me with the list." Oh, right. Check-in time from Coach Business. "What do you have going on this week? On track?"

The snow streaks over the windshield like a trip through a sci-fi space movie. There's nothing but the black road before me while the stars, er snowflakes, zoom around my trusty Toyota.

"Yeppers." I lie. Totally not on track. Packing my apartment and moving two weeks early on a whim was not on the schedule.

"Awesome. Then why the name change and refusal to answer my first question?"

I sigh because I want to tell him it's not his problem. "I don't have to explain myself to you?" That was not supposed to come out as a question, but it most certainly did.

"Is this because you're an adult?"

"Yeeesss, and I do what I want to do?"

He chuckles. "How's that working out for you?"

I inwardly grumble. There's a reason Mark is up in my business. A few years ago I asked him straight-out to help me with reaching goals and staying on track with work. For the most part, he's phenomenal. He could get a job as a life coach making big money. Thankfully I'm on the friends and family free plan. Today I wish he'd forget about this and mosey along.

"Name change. Spit it out." Coach Business does not beat around bushes.

I cave at the inevitable and spill my guts. "I think Coredelia Jane has a silliness about it. People don't take me seriously with my childish height and a name like that. Changing it to CJ should help."

"Hm." He doesn't sound convinced.

"Just say it, Mark."

"You are who you are, Cordy. Going by a different name won't change that."

"We'll see. Meanwhile..." This is the part I'm scared about. Confessing I've moved. Moving. On a whim. Decided today to pack my things and relocate two weeks before a massive work deadline right before Christmas. He's sure to nag me about that. That's something a Cordelia Jane might do. I pull in a deep breath and rush into my confession. "Diana mentioned a few days ago there's a perfectly adorable cottage for rent on the edge of Hadley Springs. And then after the breakup I didn't want to stay in Kearney anymore so I'm moving even though I have a big deadline, and it's terrible timing, but it's already done. So that's how it is." Whew. I restore my oxygen and practically yell, "Therefore, I brought everything. My car is packed tighter than your mama's spice drawer."

Mark is quiet for a beat.

"Mark?"

"I'm trying to decide if that's an innuendo for something else."

"Ahh, no. Spices? Doesn't she have a lot of them? My mom keeps hers in a drawer but it's so full that all the bonus spices are left on the counter all the time."

"Next time just say that. Don't bring *my* mom into it."

"Roger."

"That's a lot." He tut-tuts with his tongue, thinking. "Let's see. Did you check that the rental is available now?"

"I'll stay with Diana until it's ready."

"Are you going to be able to refocus quickly enough and finish the last few pages of the cookbook by your deadline?"

"Planning on it."

"Did you call Diana to tell her you're coming today and intending to stay?"

"She knows I'm coming for the holidays. We talked recently." I turn up the defrost. "Mark, I hear you rolling your eyes." The fog that had begun to creep along the edges of my windshield vanishes. "Gosh, okay. I'll call her."

I double tap the earbud before he has the chance to comment. Nosy cousin always telling me what to do...

The call to my sister rings long enough that I'm resigned to leave a chatty voicemail that she will hate. She finally answers, "This is Diana." Her straight-forward tone implies she didn't bother to look at the caller ID.

"I'm almost there!" I force the smile through my words. "Excited to see you and squish all those babies." Patches of packed snow cover parts of the road and I tap the brake to come out of cruise control.

"Hi!" My sister's voice screeches through my head and I turn the volume down. "How far out are you?"

"Just made the turn from Highway Eighty-One. Five miles?" Sudden cheers and piano music blares through the call.

"Say again?"

I clear my throat. "Five minutes tops. Are you not home?"

"Sorry, hang on." The noise fades but is still audible in the background. A baby gurgles in my ear. "Can you hear me, Cordy? Gosh, it's loud in there."

"Is that baby Jack with you?"

"You know it."

"And live music? Sounds like quite the party."

"A couple guys from church always—No! Leo, put it down. Down! You've had enough. Put it down. Don't lick —" Diana lets out an exasperated breath. "Go find Dad. Go on. And no more cookies. Fine, one more. A little one." She immediately switches from mom-voice to sister-voice. "Sorry, sis. Um. Did I miss something? What happened to next week? You're in town?"

My gas light blinks on and I do a little happy dance because I made it. Take *that*, gas meter. "I left early, and I'm trying to beat the storm. Mom warned me five times yesterday." I pitch my voice higher. "You better not be on the road when that storm hits."

"Ha! You sound just like her. No, baby. It's not for you." Jack squeals. "Ouch! Jack, quit it."

"I'm driving down your street. See you in a sec."

There seems to be a struggle on the other end. "Oh! No, Cordy. Keep going and turn left on 10th. We're at a Christmas party."

"I'm not dressed for a party. Are there cookies? Wait, no." *Keep it together, CJ!* I will not be distracted by delicious food. "I'm not party crashing."

"You're with *me*. I'm *inviting* you. And hurry. You do not want to miss the cello man. He's single. And hot."

"Too soon, Diana."

"It's never too soon to admire God's creation."

Since when are cellists hot? I immediately picture a stout man with thinning hair and a nerdy vibe who got stuck with the cello in middle school because everything else was taken, but he kept practicing because his mom made him. Thirty years later he's still single and invited to play at parties because it keeps him from always being the fifth wheel at group events. "Nah," I say. "I'll pass."

"I'm telling you, he's swoony. Even Nathan agrees."

"Oh, perfect. That's exactly what I need! A cello man that your husband thinks is hot." I fake gag. "Now I hate him on principle."

"Get over yourself, Cordy. You and Nathan have *got* to stop hating each other. It's weird and immature."

"Whatevs. I don't need a hot guy. Shaun was hot, remember?"

"Who's Shaun?" Aw, Diana is sweet when she wants to be. "Okay, it's the house with all the cars. There's a little statue of Mary and baby Jesus in the yard. See you soon."

Nope, I take it back. She's detestable. "I'll be at *your* house. I'll see you when you're all partied out."

"My house is locked."

"Good one, sis. In Hadley Springs? Don't make a liar of yourself. I'll call your bluff."

"Cordelia Jane Thompson! Quit being a dumb-dumb and get over here. It's not that kind of a party. It's a potluck thing we do every Thursday. I'm in sweatpants and there's baby drool on my shoulder. My kids are all running around like yahoos. Aaaaaaaand." She sings that word. "There's food here and none at my place. Lots and lots of food. Everyone brought something."

I sigh. I do like food. "Did you make those little ham sandwiches that are ah-may-zing and annoyingly messy with secret sauce dressing all over the bun?"

"Guess you'll have to come find out. Bye, now. They're playing one of my favorites. Got to go."

And that's how I find myself walking into a stranger's house in my grey leggings, tousled red curls in a wild bun, and green hoodie with my favorite Anne Shirley quote: *Kindred spirits are not so scarce as I used to think.* Hmm. Diana was right—I fit right in.

The large living room is crowded with a few teenagers huddled in the corner, babies on laps, men and women standing or squished together on a large wrap-around couch and a dozen folding chairs. Everyone's attention is aimed at the corner of the room. There's a man playing a full-sized keyboard, and yep, another playing the cello.

I've never seen a cello in real life. Did I mention that? It's like a fiddle but huge. When talking to Diana I realize I'd been picturing a bass, but this is smaller. There's a pointy thing about a foot long touching the floor and the rest of it fits easily between the musician's thighs. He's sitting on a stool in faded blue jeans, leather ankle boots, a V-neck black sweater pushed to his elbows, and a Santa hat.

The man moves with the music, and a foot comes off the ground as he rocks to one side. His fingers fly across the strings. He smiles at the piano guy then nods. Their upbeat version of "Oh Little Town of Bethlehem" morphs into something new. The melody is there, but it has blossomed into *more*. With perfect synchrony the musicians increase the tempo. Cello Man sweeps his gaze across the room, and Oh. My. Word.

His smile.

I'm planted in the entryway. I'm a tree in an enchanted forest and my roots grow deep. I shall not be blown over by wind or storm. My heart now beats in rhythm to the magic emanating from the man who has captured me with a grin.

His eyes lock with mine, and his fingers miss a chord. He blinks and turns his attention back to his music. The air in the room is thick. I suddenly want to escape because I don't understand this feeling. It's a mix of adoration and curiosity with a dash of boldness and a sprinkle of desire.

A fleeting baby thought reminds me of my Christmas

vow. I scowl at the back of the couch as the room erupts into applause.

You mean I can't engage in a Christmas fling with the cellist across the room?

Loud conversation fills the house and my hands have turned to fists while I watch the men pack their instruments. My leaves begin to wilt. The creek is reduced to a trickle. I have nothing to say to him. Not two hours ago I vowed to be serious. Hmmm. And why did I do that?

And focused.

That's right. I tilt my chin up. Because men don't want anything to do with a girl who can only offer punchy one-liners and cute red curls. And just like that, I'm not rooted to anything.

2

CORDELIA

GAYLA PEEVEY—I WANT A HIPPOPOTAMUS FOR CHRISTMAS

People notice me now that the show is over. Smiles and slightly confused expressions aim my direction. Before I have time to explain my intrusion, Diana barrels across the room with baby Jack in her arms. "You're here!"

Diana didn't scream an embarrassing nickname before all these strangers. See? We are grateful. I muster enough enthusiasm to match her excitement and we do a fun little hug, rock, pull back and squeal, and hug again sister dance. "Hey everyone!" She turns to the room. "This is my sister, Cordelia Thompson."

I flash a wave and fall into a mock curtsy, *Princess Diaries* style. Diana and I perfected the move as children in case we were ever called upon to take over a kingdom.

Jack is all baby softness and squishy cheeks when I bring him into my arms as a shield against anyone I don't care to meet. He honors me with an open mouthed grin and tries to yank a chunk of hair from my scalp.

"Ope. Jack, no, no, no." Diana pries his fist from my

hair. Letting go is not his favorite thing, and he twists his face into a pout.

"Gosh, Diana, this might be your cutest one yet. How old is he now? Three months? Four?"

"Six." She gives me *that* look as she draws out the word. I deserved that. Right. So it's been a few months.

"My, how time flies." Nonchalant banter isn't my strength. "Where's the rest of the gang?" Diana has five other kids here somewhere: Ten, eight, five, five, two, and Jack, who's already *six months old.*

Before she answers, Jack rubs his face against my neck and proceeds to throw up all down my front. The majority of it slides under the neck of my hoodie and into my bra. "Ahh." I shudder. "Help."

Diana bites her lips in a failed attempt not to laugh. "Sorry." She whispers with tears in her eyes.

"Oh, gosh. It's warm. Ugghhh." He wacks me in the face for good measure. I hold him away from my body. "Take it back." The smell wafts upward and I turn my head. "I'm going to your house now to shower for the rest of my life."

"No, no, no." She's laughing at me! My older sister has zero sympathy for my plight and is laughing at me. Normally I'd be laughing with her. Maybe do a hula dance and pretend it's all fun and games—grab a paper towel and make the best of it. This was nobody's fault and babies will be babies. But it's been a day and I'm done.

"Look, Diana, I'm exhausted—"

"Aunt Jewels will help you get cleaned up. You haven't even had dinner yet." She disappears with Jack.

"Aunt Cordy! Aunt Cordy!" There's an echo of high-pitched children's voices a moment before they dance around me, a human maypole.

"Hi, Lance! Hello, Leo!"

The five-year-old twins grab my hands and pull me across the house. "Come see the food! We cooked the best ones from that book you made us." Groups of partygoers move aside for the hooligans, and we land in the middle of the kitchen. Everyone else must have eaten because it's just us in here with counters full of homemade treats, chips, and veggies. The boys each hug one of my thighs, their burned red hair mops of curls. You can tell them apart because Lance has a certain quirk of his smile that is just... well, Lance. My nieces join the scene. "Happy holidays, Lauren."

Lauren's white-blond hair is tamed into a side braid. She's got her sister, Lisa, on her hip. Lisa shies away from me when I rub her back. Last visit I was her favorite. "Where's Landon?"

"He can read," says Leo.

"He likes books all'a time," says Lance. The boys eye each other and Lance says, "Now!"

One on either side, the twins squeeze my legs and try to lift me. They've attempted this trick every visit since they've been able to talk. Because I'm the size of a middle-schooler (and a small one at that) they have it in their heads they should be able to do it. What is it with people thinking they have permission to pick me up just because they can? It's always been a joke with these boys until today.

Today they manage it. For a millisecond, their joined efforts succeed, and my heels leave the floor. "Ah! Put me down. Put me down!" An awkward laugh bursts from my mouth when my feet are flat again. "You little gremlins! Get off me." But they're ruthless. Now that they know their super power, my pathetic attempt to ward them away doesn't prevail. They work as a devious machine. Leo pokes me in the side where it tickles and Lance tugs my purse. "Did you bring us treats?"

Lisa is wrapped around my ankle. When did that happen? Lauren is no help because she's filling a plate with chips and cheese sauce. If only Landon were here, maybe he'd help.

I try to wrestle free with a smile pasted on my face. Aunt Cordy is usually the fun aunt, but I don't have it in me tonight. Leo and Lance brace themselves to lift me again, and I'm not prepared for the annoyance that flares in my gut. I want to shake them off and shout at them.

One of them yells, "Go!"

My feet leave the floor with my balance off center. I tilt until I'm falling. I crash onto the tiled kitchen floor, and my head bounces against a cabinet. A ring of concerned cherub faces surrounds me. Stars dance through my vision. Little hands pat my hair, tug my shirt. I squish my eyes closed and take a moment to control my tongue from spouting something I'll regret.

"Please, stop touching me," I say through gritted teeth. A thirty pound toddler straddles my belly and pounces. "*Oof.* Lisa, not now."

"Get back." A male voice fills my ears. "Go on, Lance. Leo, move over."

I open my eyes as Lisa's weight vanishes. Kneeling before me is the cello man. His jovial smile has been replaced with concern, maybe pity. He bounces Lisa on his knee, and the twins hover on either side of him. "Lauren." He speaks without moving his gaze from me. "Take the kids out of the kitchen."

3

CORDELIA

TCHAIKOVSKY—DANCE OF THE SUGAR PLUM FAIRY

"I'm fine." I ignore his outstretched hand and scoot until my back rests against the cabinet. The white speckled floor-tile is littered with chip crumbs and dark splotches near the coffee bar. Ignoring the smell of baby puke that hovers around me, I unwind the white scrunchie from my mess of curls and tenderly run my fingers along the back of my head.

"You good?" He's still crouched in front of me, but I avoid his gaze.

"I said I was fine." I don't want to acknowledge his presence. I don't want to be here. I certainly don't want to think about how a few of my favorite kids got the best of me. I'm extremely close to tears. *Can everyone please go away so I can cry?!*

"Is it a crime to be concerned for your wellbeing?" His voice is soft, not unkind. The sweetness of his statement does not help the impending waterworks situation.

"I get it, but I don't need your help." What I need is for

17

him to get lost so he doesn't see me completely fall apart. "Thank you." *Please, please go away.* "I could have handled it."

I shouldn't be rude to him. He hasn't done anything. But being assaulted by a pack of kids is bad enough without having a witness. I feel small. My highest desire is to crawl into a tunnel until everyone forgets about me and then emerge as a brilliant, bold, beautiful woman and start all over again. Who do I call to make this happen? Where's the magnet with that hotline? I rest my forehead on my knees and my thick hair curtains on either side. It's almost as nice as a cave in here. I think I'll stay. Bye. See you in the spring.

He releases a sigh that reflects my posture. "Come on. Let's get you off the floor." He rests a hand on my arm that I've wrapped around my knees. "I'd hate for another parade to come through for cookies and trample you in their wake."

I swat his hands away, and he stands. *Don't poke the bear. She's hibernating!* Lauren and the kids have disappeared. The man raises an eyebrow and leans a hip against the counter, arms crossed. He dips his hand into a bowl of red and green M&M's. After tossing one into his mouth, he takes a shot at me and it bounces off the top of my head. When I don't react he does it again. "Why don't you open your mouth? You're wasting good chocolate."

I narrow my eyes and flinch when a red covered bite of chocolate hits me square on the chin. "Why don't you *grow up*?" That'll teach him. My cheek twitches into an almost smile. It takes everything in me not to fish the candy from the floor and throw it back at him. But I've just been overcome by a few children, and I refuse to act like one myself. "Don't you have somewhere else to be?"

My less-than-holiday-spirit vibes are strong. I climb to my feet and help myself to a bowl of potato chips at my elbow. Chips are better than caves. I yank my scrunchie from my wrist and wrestle my mane into a twisted bun high on my head. His gaze tracks the movements of my hands, and he doesn't answer me. "Well?"

He bites into a brownie. "You could wear it down. It's cute."

Sure, that's exactly what I want right now. To be *cute.* No! So much for my Christmas vow. I lift my chin and wrap a loose curl around the bun and tuck it in.

The rest of the brownie disappears into his mouth, and he dances both hands over his head with fingers splayed.

"Is that supposed to be me? Rude." I own that my hair is a mess. When I haven't been in the car all day, I add a ton of mousse and set it free. It hangs halfway down my back and twists and turns every which way. It's wild and fun and I love it. He has no right to make fun of my hair. "Okay, I think we're done here." I turn to find Diana and tell her I'm leaving.

"Wait." He halts me with a touch to my shoulder. "I'm sorry. I wasn't trying to insult you."

My bottom lip quivers, and I smash down the offending twitch with my fingers. I SHALL NOT CRY.

"Oh, gosh." His eyes grow wide. "Please, don't... I'm sorry. It's beautiful. Really. So red and shiny. Here." He steps closer. I don't move, and he doesn't ask before reaching behind my head to remove the scrunchie. The whole mess tumbles around my shoulders. My face is level with his chest as he fluffs the sides and adjusts curls. He smells like tropical coconut and something earthy. "There."

My voice braves the thick atmosphere, but in my attempt to hold in my embarrassing emotions it comes out sharp and cruel. "Why did you do that?"

"Don't move." He fiddles with his cell phone and holds

it up to me. "See?" On the screen is a snapshot of my face. My hair isn't cute. It's... dramatic. It's lush beach vibes. Corkscrews and waves that say to the world, "I *dare you* to keep me locked away." I look almost haunted. Freckles stark against pale skin. Icy green eyes that shine with unshed tears. They are wide and intense. They are either planning to murder you or would swear on pain of death to keep your darkest secret. I've never seen such a serious picture of myself.

His nose crinkles and his gaze strays to my chest and lower. At first I think he's inappropriately checking me out, but then he points at my collar. "Jack?"

"Oh." I'd momentarily forgotten that I was a walking vessel of baby puke.

"I'll find Aunt Jewels." He pockets the phone. "You need to eat this." An oatmeal butterscotch cookie hangs in front of my face. I bring in a shaky breath.

"Open," he says.

I narrow my eyes and snatch the cookie. "I can feed myself."

A beautiful smirk lights his face. "There we go. Be right back."

Before I finish the cookie, an elderly woman in a gold silk blouse and green felt skirt that brushes the floor pops up by my elbow as if summoned from a lamp. She offers a hand. "Jewel Conner. Aunt Jewels to everyone except my doctor. Welcome to my home. I'm so glad you made it in time." She's wearing a pair of red vintage cat glasses, full-sized red ornaments as big as tennis balls hang from her ears, and a necklace of wooden figures representing the entire nativity rattle together as she moves. She follows my gaze.

"You like my necklace? My nephew carved these for

me. I'm sure he intended for me to hang them on the tree, but I'm a rebel. Have you eaten yet, dear?" She wraps my hand in both of hers. "You're freezing. Did you forget your coat? Don't tell me you're one of those tough kids who never wears them. There's no such thing as bad weather, only bad clothing." I'm guided to the counter of food and she begins filling a holiday themed paper plate. "On a day like today, you're in bad clothing if you don't want to freeze your patootie off when you walk back to the car. I'll lend you my shawl when it's time." Bacon wrapped peppers, a handful of crackers, a slice from a cheese ball. "At the very least we'll have my nephew heat your car for you first." She winks, hand paused over Diana's ham sandwiches. "He'll start your car. That's all I meant, darling. Now, hon. No need to look so confused. He's a very nice man. I saw you watching him when you came in. Glued you to the floor." A sprinkle of M&M's like an artist's final brush stroke is added to the plate. "Was it his smile or the music?"

She leans in and lowers her voice. "He has that effect on people, and I'm not convinced it's the cello. His father was the same way. He's single again. Not his father." She laughs at her own joke. "Diana tells me you've just had another breakup. You poor dear, but all for the best I'm sure. Now, hon. Eat." She holds the plate to me.

"Oh, okay." I swallow, not sure if I'm allowed to speak. "Actually, I'm..." I motion to my hoodie where the mess has seeped through to the outside.

"Ope." The midwest slang slips without thought from her lips. "I see, yes. Did Jack get you? I never hold the kid. I gave up on him months ago. Fool me once—You're a 34B? 32?"

My hand is no longer mine. She tugs me down the hallway and away from the noise of the party. I follow like a trained dog on a leash held by a toddler. She has the soft, almost translucent skin of someone who's spent more time on this earth than I can comprehend. I could pull away, but she's just so darn cute—and expectant—I follow by choice.

Once we're in an old-fashioned bedroom with wooden furniture from the Victorian era, she releases my hand and sets the plate on the dresser. She pulls me into a side hug. "I'm Jewel Conner and I'm so glad you're here. You're going to call me Aunt Jewels. I'm told you're Cordelia Thompson and I don't know you yet, but you're in my home and that means you are my guest. I like you. What's your middle name?"

"Um, Jane. I go by CJ." It sounds foreign on my tongue, but I'm sticking with it.

"I don't think so, dear." She moves around the room in a calm dance while humming "Joyful, Joyful We Adore Thee." My arms are soon filled with a soft pair of gray leggings, a ribbed undershirt, and a thick purple sweatshirt with a sugar plum fairy and plastic emblems of candies sewn into it. Aunt Jewels vanishes into the master bathroom and the sound of running water overtakes her song.

"Now, hon, you help yourself." Her head appears in the doorway. "What are you doing over there? Sticky feet? You're a sight. How long was your drive today?"

"Only about three hours. I packed and cleaned my place first. My room, at least. I shared the apartment with three other girls."

"Diana tells me you're moving to town for a while. That's wonderful news. The perfect cottage has been waiting for you. We'll talk about that when you're done." She guides me into the bathroom. A deep soaking tub is already half filled. "Look along the side there. I have salts, bath oils, bubbles. The last covered dish is packed with dried rose petals. Take your pick."

I find my voice. "This is too much. If you'll hand me a wash rag or a paper towel—"

"Poppycock. I didn't pay a small fortune to remodel my bathroom to keep it all to myself. When's the last time you soaked in a tub?"

"Um..." I dip my eyebrows.

"Thought so. You stay in until the water cools. Don't worry about a thing, Cordelia Jane. When you get out, take a nap on the bed if you've a mind."

I try to say thank you, but when I open my mouth I realize how close to falling apart I really am. Who is this woman? She behaves as if we're intimately connected, but it doesn't feel like an intrusion.

Aunt Jewels pauses on her way out and takes in my face. She clicks her tongue and wraps me in a hug. "Oh, sweet thing. It's going to be all right."

"I'm sorry," I whisper. "I don't know why I'm so sad." Where did that come from? I don't know this woman. Yet I lean into her embrace in a way I haven't done with anyone in years. How can she, who I met less than five minutes ago, have this kind of power over me?

"You don't have to know why." Her arms strengthen around me. "Sometimes when the soul is at work the body can't keep up. You've moved away from the familiar, things are changing, you're at a party with strangers." She holds my face between her soft hands. "You expected safety and comfort, and instead you're surrounded by people who don't know you and then a baby ruins your adorable outfit. Besides, you've recently escaped a serious relationship?"

I choke a laugh at *escaped.*

"Does that cover it?"

I glance at her with a smile. She might officially be the most wonderful woman ever. Where's the hidden camera? How did she put into words even things I wasn't aware of? She only left out the fall in the kitchen.

She raises her hand in farewell. "I'm going to find Gilbert and tell him about the pretty girl who's just arrived. He's single, you know."

My eyes have to be bugging out of my head. "Gilbert? There's a Gilbert here?" The rest of her statement sinks in. "Oh, don't tell him that. Don't tell him anything. Of course, that's so sweet of you to say, but I don't want to make it weird for him."

There's a Gilbert at this party. I've been waiting for Gilbert—I know it's only symbolic. I've been waiting for a *metaphorical* Gilbert. *Come on, CJ, you don't need a literal man named Gilbert.* A rose is a rose and by any other name would smell as sweet, or—but, if the slipper fits. Don't ask, don't ask, *don't ask.*

"Is he cute?" Yes, I asked.

"Oh, hon. He's a dream, but you already know this. We've been talking about him all evening. Gilbert is my nephew. The one on the cello."

Sweet smiles, soul wrenching music, flying M&M's. I was talking to Gilbert the whole time? Flames erupt from my chest and burst along my neck and face. I cover my cheeks with my hands that are now slick with clammy sweat. "We met in the kitchen. I was rude to him." *Wait.* "Your actual nephew?" If everyone is supposed to call her Aunt Jewels, how is this not confusing?

She laughs, hand on the bathroom door handle.

"He's a teddy bear. I doubt he remembers it the way you do. Clean up and reset yourself." She points. "Leave the soiled clothes in the hamper there. The sugar plum sweatshirt is thick enough you won't need a bra with those tiny boobs. Nobody will notice. I don't want to see you for at least an hour." She pushes up her sleeve and checks the time on a watch face wider than her wrist. "The young families will be gone by then. We'll have the games and cards out for the rest of us. I'll tell Diana I've got you."

"I can run to my car and grab a change of clothes." I'm flattered but also uncomfortable. Where will people think I've disappeared to? I've never bathed mid-party before.

"You're in my home, Cordelia, and I insist. You're loved and accepted here."

On her way out she taps a CD player on the bathroom counter and soft piano mixed with ambient sounds fills the air. Then she pauses, looking at me expectantly. I wait, eyebrows raised, until a cello joins the piano and her face splits into a knowing smile.

"There," she says. "You just try not to relax with that flowing through your veins."

I could try. But have you ever tried to relax with the knowledge flowing through your veins that a certain cello man named Gilbert, with a smile that melts chocolate, is on the other side of the house?

4

GILBERT

"There's a pretty new girl in town, Gilbert." Aunt Jewels fairly bursts with the secret she's about to share when I finally spot her exiting the hallway from her bedroom. We must have missed each other, and she's already helped the girl from the kitchen.

"She's pretty new? Or new and pretty?" I offer my elbow and escort her toward the living room.

"Both." She absently adjusts her ridiculous nativity necklace. I'm glad I didn't carve the figurines any bigger. Should've known she'd turn them into jewelry. "She's delightful. You will simply love her." My aunt's commentary is spot on, although I would have added that the girl is also overwhelmed and tired. Delightfully snippy.

"Should I schedule the proposal for next weekend?" I smile when she continues to fiddle with Mary and Joseph. She never makes eye contact when she's scheming. "Remember what we talked about last week? I have deadlines. Goals. Plans. I don't need you to set me up. Just

26

because I'm single doesn't mean I'm lonely." I could leave it at that, but it's so much fun to poke the bear. "I've sworn off women forever."

She shoots me a glance over her red-rimmed glasses. "That's a lie from the pit, and you know it, son. Kinsey wasn't for you. Try again."

"Kinsey? Are we still on that?" Kinsey and I broke up months ago. We were barely an item in the first place. "Fine." I gently remove the manger with baby Jesus from her grasp and arrange the figures to hang in a proper line. "Give me two years. Can I do this my own way? I need a couple more years to focus on the big house. You've seen it, Aunt J. You know it's going to be worth a fortune, but I have to do the work. The full-time, overcommitted work. I don't have time to date until I've sold it and have my feet under me when I tackle the next."

"Honey, you're all alone out there—"

"Don't." I run both hands through my hair. "How can you possibly say that? John and I are hired out at least once a month. I'm here right now! I'm at your party every Thursday. I'm at church on Sunday, I rub shoulders with people at the hardware store, and you wouldn't believe how often I'm hauling a trailer from Omaha. Home Depot, Menards, Lowes? I know all the managers by name. Carl, Katie, Sam. We're practically water cooler buddies. Not alone." I laugh with a huff. "No one gets lonely with you for an Aunt."

"Now, hon." She guides me to a quiet corner away from the card tables being set up on the other end. "You don't have to be lonely to enjoy the company of a wife."

"You're meddling again." It's our broken record conversation again.

"What if your forever girl is here, and you miss her because you're wearing blinders?"

There is no arguing with Aunt Jewels. "Woe is me."

"I worry about you."

"I'm great, and I don't have time for a girl with my workload."

"You will always have work!" She tosses her hands to the side. "You'll finish this house and sell it, and you'll find another. What difference does it make?"

"I can't afford to date. It's not worth my—*Bah.*" I don't need to defend myself to her again. She's heard me explain how this process works. She's the one who's blind to my logic. My hands come together under my nose, chin resting on my thumbs while I contemplate our circulatory conversation. Aunt Jewels wants me to meet the cute girl I've already met. I have no qualms with this, but I refuse to be shoved into a relationship. Especially when it's not what I want.

Considering our kitchen interaction, I'm sure that chick isn't looking for a relationship with me either. I admit she's intriguing. She's fiery and exciting. My attention riveted to her the moment she walked into the house. Goodness, she's the first chord I've missed mid-show in years. That's something. I draw in a breath and refocus.

I will not have an extra minute or penny until I sell the house I'm flipping. Dating is a distraction. Dating is expensive. This property took all of my savings. The construction loan is a heavy burden, and what I scrape in for my part-time music is barely enough to eat. My time is too valuable to waste it showering some girl with time and money I simply don't have. I won't bring a girlfriend, much less a wife, into that mess.

Aunt Jewels meets my stare.

She opens her mouth, but after a stern shake of my head, she shuts it. Kinsey and I drifted apart for this very reason. I could never afford to go to the places she wanted to go. She needed more time than I could give her to make it work. Why spin that record again?

Once my pulse decrescendos, I lower my hands with a slow exhale. "Even you wouldn't want me to acquire a girl-friend and not treat her how she deserves."

"But, Gil—"

"I love you, but stop."

"You never did like being told what to do." She raises a chin in challenge.

I chuckle. "Did Cam call you? He texted that he'll be in town sometime next week."

"No, he hasn't. Your brother never remembers to check in with me. I'll call him."

"Would you? There's no room at my place this time."

I wiggle out of any more confrontations and take my cello to the truck. On the way back, I catch John hauling his keyboard out. "Good show." I meet him along the sidewalk.

He raises a fist, and I knock mine against it. "What was up with you? If I didn't know better, I'd say Diana's sister bewitched you."

"Who?"

"Cordy Thompson. Cordelia. That ginger you couldn't keep your eyes from."

"*That's* the sister?" I shove my hands in my jean pockets against the cold. "I didn't recognize her. I'd only seen pictures when Diana showed everyone her skydiving thing forever ago."

"Yeah. I was just talking to Nate. I guess she's moving in for a few weeks. Maybe helping out with the kids?"

"Isn't she a chef?"

John shrugs. "Food photography? I don't know if you have to be a chef for that."

"Huh. Cool. Hey, I liked those arpeggios you dropped into 'Silent Night.'"

"Thanks." His face lights up with a smile. "I'm so bored of that song. I had to do something to stay awake."

The icy snow crunches under my boots. "That'd go viral for sure. 'Man faints during boring Christmas show.'"

He stands the keyboard case on its end. "Speaking of viral, you check our channel recently?"

"Never. Watching myself play weirds me out."

"Gil, buddy. This is how we're going to make it big. It wouldn't hurt to get involved in the marketing. Hadley Strings has a chance to get out of here if we'd push around the edges."

"You have your hobbies. I have mine."

John sighs. "It's not a hobby if it makes us real money someday."

"What if we did a mashup with 'Silent Night'? Flip it on its head with... 'Go Tell it on the Mountain.'" It's ironic because the songs are saying two different things with the same overarching message.

"Sure. You write it. I'll play it."

Light pours through the picture window of the living room. People look like they're having a good time. "Well, hey. I'm gonna take off."

"All work and no play—" John slips on the ice, and I grab his elbow to steady him.

"I played all afternoon, and it was great. I'll see you Saturday."

His face falls. "You're not staying for games again? I miss you in there. There is no replacement."

"Dream team for sure. Some other time, man." I slap him on the back and run inside to say good-bye to Aunt Jewels. I can't afford another late night and therefore lose another early morning. With the amount of work that needs done on the big house before January, I can't give myself breaks.

When I asked John's sister, Nicole, to keep her ears open for a renter to my small cottage, where I currently sleep, I thought I'd have more time. She sees dozens of patients a day at her family clinic. Everyone tells her everything. If someone was looking for a place to rent, she'd hear of it. Magically, she told me this afternoon she'd found a renter wanting the place right after the holidays. Too desperate for the income, I won't turn it down even if it means working around the clock the next two weeks before Christmas.

After I arrive at my little shack of a house, I sit in my truck an extra minute with 80s rock music filling the cab.

Why don't you grow up? Cordelia's statement didn't sting. I shake my head in a silent laugh. There was no bite in it. Nathan's kids were ruthless, and I could tell she was embarrassed.

I repeat the question out loud, "Why don't you grow up, Gil Conner?" Great question. *Never.* I'll be a little boy forever. Peter Pan for life. I chuckle and kill the engine but wait to open the door while the chorus repeats of The Cars' "Just What I Needed." My breath billows around me fogging the windows. And my nose is about frozen. The two miles from my Aunt's house to mine isn't far enough to get the heat moving. The temperature has continued to drop all day. Last I checked we were in the single digits.

Holiday parties are my favorite. I get paid to play. Paid to eat. Sometimes I travel to gigs at ritzy art galas or estate parties where I'm expected to play softly in the background and slink away when my shift ends. Those are okay. Music is music and I love it, but nothing beats parties where people *want* to hear the music. They can't help but feel its pull and they're sucked into my world. I relish when their bodies begin to move all on their own as if their spirit is captured by the song and they're no longer in control.

Christmas parties in my hometown? A blast, especially when I'm allowed an exit whenever I want. It almost feels wrong to take the money. I do, though. My bills won't pay themselves. Bills, bills, bills. Time to get out of this truck and make a plan for work tomorrow.

Man, that girl was quirky. Nathan never mentioned his sister-in-law was so cute.

I tug my hat lower over my ears and grab the foil-wrapped plate of leftovers that Aunt Jewels forced upon me. A smidgen of self-pity slithers into my chest for how I live nearly the exact same life I've lived since I was eighteen. Play music. Swing a hammer. Make a little money. Beg food from Aunt Jewels.

She met me at the door with the food. I kissed her on the cheek, and I said thanks. It will sustain me another day. *When are you going to grow up?*

Never! I refuse. Just to prove it, I slip a cookie from under the foil and shove the whole thing in my mouth.

I tap my fingers on the steering wheel while I mentally gird my loins to open the door and step into the tundra. The snow continues to fall, and the wind whips it around with such violent anger that it doesn't have time to settle. With a warrior's cry I grab my food and open the door, which cuts the music. My cell vibrates my coat pocket with Bach's Cello Suite No. 1. I slide back on the bench and slam the door. "Conner."

"Hi! Gil. Hey." It's Nicole. "You made it home already? Good. Good. So, listen. Hey. I know it's short notice. I didn't catch you before you left. Royce cornered me. He's determined to convince me of his next conspiracy. Did you know the government has alien technology powering their stealth flyers?"

"He explained it yesterday at the grocery. Between the yogurt and sour cream."

"Mm. So you're up to speed."

I push down the old metal lock on the door and pull it up again. Down. Up. "Anything else?"

"I confirmed your renter! You've moved out of the cottage already, I hope."

"I—"

"Your room in the big house is ready to go?"

"Sure, but—"

"Wonderful!"

I let her interruptions slide. It's not like what I have to say will make a difference. My bedroom is almost ready. But I can complete it in a few days. A week at most. Even though I told her I had sleeping quarters for myself in the big house, I've spent most of my construction time focused on the cottage since it's warmer there.

"This is simply wonderful. I was hoping you'd say that. I know how busy you are with your music. It seems you and John are out every weekend for a show." She releases a sigh with a feminine laugh at the end. "Thank heavens. Good. That's good."

"When's our guy moving in?" I wait for her to tell me after the holidays like we've already talked about and make this phone call unnecessary. As planned, I'll finish my room, install the water heater, and at least get the shower working with a few days left to enjoy Christmas before he moves in. "Did they finally hire a band teacher for the school?"

"She, actually. She's coming tonight."

"Mmmm." I cover my annoyance with a deep breath.

This is what I get for asking my best friend's sister to do something I should have done myself, even if she does have better connections. This is unexpected on multiple levels.

Merry Christmas to all.

Shoot. "Guess I better pack my toothbrush. She probably doesn't want that in her new bathroom. When should I expect her?" It's currently past eight o'clock.

Silence on the other end. "Nickie? Nicole? When's she coming?" I glance at the screen. My phone is dead. *Double shoot.* I had a full battery when I answered. Phone batteries aren't designed for single digit weather.

"Wonderful!" I shove another cookie in my mouth feeling anything but wonderful. "Awesome!" Chew. Swallow. Unknown she-guest arriving at any moment. I get to move out of my snuggly warm cottage in weather so cold that electronics are dying. I have an unfinished bedroom in my unfinished house. I need to build a fire in the big house. I need to pack my meager possessions. We got this. "Let's do this!" I Tarzan-pummel my chest.

Knowing I'll return, I leave my plate of food and launch myself into the cold. I run around to the other side and grab my baby, where I've carefully shoved her case into the passenger seat. She shouldn't be left out here in the cold.

Once inside the cottage, I start the timer on my watch. Me against myself. I will win. But how quickly? I throw my dirty laundry, shoes, a deck of cards, books, and a few odds and ends onto my bed—*her* bed—and pull the sheets into an I'm-running-for-the-hills bundle and shove the rest of my clothes into my rolly suitcase. I fill my now-empty laundry basket with everything that belongs to me in the kitchen— not much. I hesitate over my cello and leave her in the closet. I'll come back for her once the big house is warmer.

Small puddles form as the snow I've tracked inside

begins to melt. *Tick, tick, tick.* She could be coming down the driveway this very moment. I ransack the bathroom and haul everything to my truck. Back inside, I swish a damp rag over everything in the bathroom and the kitchen counter.

The gleaming wood of the new butcherblock taunts me. This morning I rubbed the seventh layer of linseed oil into my masterpiece. I run a calloused finger along the edge and hold in the sigh trying to escape. I spent far too much time arranging the planks to make sure the slight variance in color was artfully random. "Someday, Gil." Someday, I'd finish a job and keep it.

Once I slide into the truck I stop my timer. Twenty-two minutes. Not bad at all. Winners get another cookie. Cheers to me.

The big house, as we lovingly call her, is a shell. She's been gutted to the bones. The classic Victorian has electricity running to all the outlets but only a few overhead lights. There's a working toilet but no shower. A spigot in the kitchen but no hot water.

Did I mention no central heating yet? Sure, there's an open fireplace on the main floor and in each of the three upstairs bedrooms, but have you ever tried to heat a mansion with fireplaces? It would require servants. Plural. There's a reason "woodcutter" used to be an occupation. The space heater is trained on the pipes in the kitchen to keep my water in liquid form.

She's an old *old* royal beauty. With missing teeth and bald patches. A hag. But she's getting a facelift. That's why I bought her.

Gilbert Conner will fix it.

Gilbert Conner, handy-man extraordinaire!

Gilbert Conner, the frozen musician whose fingers have morphed into unfeeling stumps of flesh that drop three matches in a pathetic attempt to light the kindling. "Come on, darling." I speak sweetly to the fourth match. "This is your show now. You're on."

She strikes true. In building up the fire I pretend that I'm not at all anxious as to whom my new renter will be across the driveway, and ponder why the possibility of a female renter had never previously entered my mind.

CORDELIA

JOHN DENVER AND THE MUPPETS—DECK THE HALLS

B*ing!*
I emerge from the frothy bubbles that smell like orange juice and vanilla. What magic is this?

Careful not to drop my lifeline into the bath, I swipe a wet finger across the screen.

> Diana: We went home! Aunt J says you're in the bath??? What a crazy girl you are. Jack really did a number on you, huh.

> > Cordelia: It was against my will. I put up a fight. Noooooo don't make me take a bath in your luxurious tub fit for royalty.

> > Cordelia: Have you seen this place?

> Diana: I have. She kidnapped me on my birthday and had a spa day for me and friends.

> > Cordelia: Ohhh. I remember this, I didn't realize that was a local thing.

Diana: You thought we'd gone to a legit spa????

Cordelia: Um.

Diana: *GIF of baby throwing money out of a window.*

Cordelia: Do I want to know how many different naked people have been in this tub?

Diana: Would clothed people make you feel better about it?

Cordelia: Possibly.

Diana: She hires a weekly cleaning service. You're golden.

Typing bubbles appear and disappear beside her name.

Cordelia: So I'll see you later?

Diana: About that... don't freak out.

Cordelia: Now I'm freaking out. You can't lead with that!!

No texts come through, just the appearance of more typing bubbles that disappear again.

Cordelia: KILLIN ME. SHORTER TEXTS. SEND NOW.

Diana: I'm convinced that Jack isn't sick, it's just regular baby stuff, but

Diana: The twins threw up in the car on the way home.

Cordelia: Gasp!!

Diana: Nathan's out there now trying to scrape it up before it freezes to the seats. GAG.

Diana: I've showered the boys and they're in bed, I'm nursing Jack and he feels a little warm. But Landon is already asleep and he NEVER goes down early.

Cordelia: Noooo... Pray tell DID YOU INFECT THE WHOLE TOOOOWWWN?

Diana: I feel nauseous, but it might be because I've helped change clothes and dealt with all the nasty...???

Cordelia: Boo! Noooooo!

Diana: So...

Cordelia: I'll sleep under the bridge, thanks.

Diana: Right, so you need to talk to Dr. Nicole Brader.

Cordelia: I'm not sick YET!

Diana: Quit it.

Diana: Nickie is the one arranging the house you were going to rent, she's still at the party. Remember how you were going to stay with me the next two weeks?

Cordelia: Uh, yes. I haven't forgotten...

Diana: Yea, K. So I already talked with her. She says you can move in tonight and then if we're lucky Jack didn't spread too much love and you'll escape whatever might be happening over here.

Cordelia: SIGGGHHHH. Whhhhyyyy are your kids always sick?

Diana: I'm going to pretend you didn't say that and you're not thinking about your poor self sleeping in a quiet house then getting up when you want and not because someone needs you to clean up a bodily fluid.

Diana: You'll also enjoy watching an entire show without interruption, maybe drink your morning coffee while it's still hot? You're MORE than welcome to stay at my place and help manage puke through the night, change soiled sheets, rock feverish babies.

Diana: YOUR CHOICE

Cordelia: Sorry.

Diana: That's right you are. So I'll check in later.

Diana: And there goes Lauren. Crap.

Diana: Bye love ya. gtg

Cordelia: YOUCANDOHARDTHINGS. I love you!

With damp hair in a bun and sporting my new favorite borrowed sweatshirt, I play games for two hours with about a dozen others while Aunt Jewels washes and dries my clothes. She pumps us full of the most amazing peppermint hot chocolate—and no matter how desperately I beg her for the recipe she won't give it up. She keeps calling us "kids" which is funny since she's lumped Mr. and Mrs. Nilsson in that label, and they must be at least mid-fifties.

This is the most relaxed yet stimulating party I've ever attended. Nobody acts weird about "getting to know the new girl" but also nobody ignores me. It's as if they all said, "Oh, hey! CJ's here. Cool, cool. Let's play games." And yes, I've been introducing myself as CJ. I think it fits my new self better than Cordelia. CJ is chill. More focused. A little serious. She's not as whimsical and impulsive as Cordelia.

I totally play it cool about Gilbert Conner and the fact that his name is Gilbert. It helps that he left before I returned to the party, refreshed from my bath. Most of the people hadn't seen me before the Jack fiasco and are none the wiser that I've been naked across the house. Sorry to fixate on this, but until you've taken a bath in a stranger's house in the middle of a party, I'm not sure you can fully understand.

Because I have the self-control of a stalking tiger, I don't ask any direct questions about Gilbert. Yes, I linger before the framed photo of a smiling Gilbert and another young man with Aunt Jewels on the mantle. And then the gold-framed one next to it of him playing the cello. And the artistic black-and-white shot of him and John, the piano guy, performing on a stage with a single spotlight overhead. Very artsy, that one. But then! There's the photo of him PLAYING WITH A PUPPY in the hallway. But I don't think anyone notices my snagged attention.

I've put together a mental list of everything I know about this Gilbert.

- The actual nephew of Aunt Jewels (my new favorite woman in the whole wide world). She never had children, and Gilbert and his brother Cameron are the sons of her eighteen-years-younger kid brother.
- A teddy bear—per her description.
- Owner of the cottage I'm moving into tonight. And I've since learned through extremely subtle investigative work that he's a contractor who buys and flips houses, plays the cello *and* piano at events all over Nebraska and even records his own original music!
- Also, his name is Gilbert.
- Gilbert Conner.
- *Hello*, Handsome.

With these important details in place, I replay the scene in the kitchen. I was unwelcoming due to my awkward embarrassment over my almost-crying and all the mess I'd been through today, but he didn't run away. In contrast, he tried to cheer me up. So... I think I'll get another chance.

Yes, I have an insane amount of work to do in order to meet my publishing deadline by December twenty-second. But a girl can dream—and I do—about moving into a *cottage* next to the epitome of everything I'll ever need in a man.

Dramatic much?

Uh, no. I've been waiting for a Gilbert Blythe my whole life, although I had pictured it differently—perhaps a wealthy doctor (with lots of side smiles who says "sorry" in a funny British accent). Since it's too late to have met a sweetheart during my school years who waits patiently for me to accept his love and then writes me letters over a year of courtship while I teach at a boarding school for girls and work on my craft as a writer, Gilbert Conner, cello man and landlord/contractor is sufficient.

Have I mentioned how excited I am to see this cottage everyone keeps talking about? Cottage *screams* adorable. I'm told it has butcher block countertops and a farm-style white sink. It will be perfect for staging the photos I need for finishing my *Christmas Comforts* cookbook.

We play a dangerous few games of spoons until Nickie —aka Dr. Nicole Brader—and I both have an iron grip on the same white plastic spoon. A fight to the death may have ensued if the spoon hadn't just broken between our combined efforts. We triumphantly raise our respective ends of the spoon.

Nickie high-fives me and we hip bump and victory dance while the others cheer. The noise of our celebration drowns the slow croons of Elvis having a blue Christmas from the speaker on the mantle. We finish the game, and Aunt Jewels tells us that it's almost midnight and if we don't go home she'll turn us all into pumpkins.

"Your clothes, hon." She hands me a cloth sack that is suspiciously heavier than one outfit. When I attempt to look inside she smacks my hand. "Later."

"Ouch. Okay."

She insists it's not too late to call Gilbert and let him know I'm on my way over. I refuse to make the call at eleven forty-five. If he's been told I'm coming tonight, I have no fear about being locked out. There's no reason to disturb him at midnight. Of course, I add his contact information to my phone—including his address which just happens to be *my* new address. Feels scandalous.

I do a little happy dance on the inside because this is the FIRST real life Gilbert I have ever met, and *I have his number*.

Merry Christmas to all. Who was sad? Not me. This evening has been nothing but one big gift since I successfully tamped down any earlier emotions regarding Shaun (Who's he?) the breakup, moving across the state, relocating...

Matt Wilder's "Break My Stride" runs through my head as I slip and slide across the icy driveway to my car. Ain't nothing gonna bring me down tonight after that spa treatment, hot chocolate from heaven, games with new friends that are amazing, a new grandma, and *Gilbert's number saved in my phone.*

CORDELIA

FRIDAY, DECEMBER 15

BING CROSBY—I'LL BE HOME FOR CHRISTMAS

I t's nearing one in the morning and I'm still wired. Once I searched the lyrics to "Break My Stride"—because that one line kept bouncing from the sides of my brain like a free pinball machine—I was less enthused about life in general. Basically, the song's about how this girl is going to remain single forever. *Errrmkay.* A bit of a joykill.

Infatuations aside, this cottage is not everything I'd dreamed. If you're picturing Snow White's little cabin in the woods with the thatched roof, you're close. But do you remember the state of the place when she found it? With the cobwebs and the random furniture? Squeaky doors? Dripping faucets?

Thankfully it was warm-ish when I entered my new home. Gilbert must have dropped by earlier and turned the heat up for me—that is, he switched on a fancy space heater with rollers and a faux iron grill and wooden paneling. According to the red numbers on the display, it's now sixty-five degrees in the kitchen.

I carried in three boxes of my photography equipment and another two of kitchen what-nots. I'm pumped to get things organized so I can work tomorrow.

As I haul myself onto the counter to wipe seventy-three years of dust from the cabinet shelves with my green earbuds in place, my call goes through to Mark. It's only eleven p.m. in Phoenix... much too late for respectful or civilized people.

I'm neither.

"This had better be important." He answers with weak, slurred words. Maybe I woke him this time.

"Mark! You were right. Renting this cottage might be the worst, most impulsive decision I've ever made."

He groans as one might while rolling over in bed. "Aside from the decision to move across the state earlier today?"

"That one didn't seem so bad because my plan was to crash at Diana's."

"Whatever, because you love to be woken by a pack of kids at dawn." He stifles a yawn. "How and where were you going to work at Diana's?"

"Mark, staaahhhp, I know. That's why I'm here instead. Renting a cottage. You prove my point entirely. The idea of a *cottage* was so charming." I swipe at a dust bunny that looks ready to sprout fangs. "How was I to know it was a crumbling beast?"

His quiet laugh comforts me through my neon earbuds. "Really? I thought it was a tiny one-bedroom hovel. I'm looking it up." My cousin's positive energy comes through the call like it always does. He doesn't berate me for waking him up, and I relax into the familiarity of our relationship.

"It was an under the table deal." I blow a stray hair from my eyes. "Word of mouth. Friend of a friend. You won't find it posted anywhere."

"Have you paid anything for it yet? Just move out."

"Diana's kids were sick and I desired to avoid the plague. Besides, I signed the papers for twelve months and handed over a check for the security deposit and first month's rent this evening."

His chuckle turns into a burst of laughter.

"Okay, Mark." I chuck my rag into the sink and squat near the faucet to rinse it out. His laughter increases at my admonishment. "You can stop. Haha, so funny. Layers of dirt on the shelves I can handle. It's not as bad as I made it sound."

"You signed a twelve-month lease sight unseen?"

"Have you looked at available real estate for Hadley Springs? There's *nothing* near Hadley Springs."

He fills the pause with a tongue clicking rhythm that sounds suspiciously like "Deck the Halls."

"Aha," he says. "Found one. There's a studio above a garage... oh, no. You do not want that place."

I shake out my rag and refold it before shuffling along the counter to the next shelf. "I saw that one. Besides the obvious ax murderer living below, it's still forty miles from Diana. I may as well move to Omaha if I'm not going to be near family. I want the quaint village, Mark. I'm in my Anne Girl era, and I need to set the stage."

He chimes in with the appropriate "I'm listening but don't care" hums on the other end.

"I'll have to embrace an insane amount of floor scrubbing. Maybe I'm in a Marilla Cuthbert era instead. This cottage is like a lemur. You say 'aww' and want to pet it until you remember it's still a wild animal." My once white dishcloth is gray and I dump it into the sink again. "Then it comes at you with its mouth open and you get a momentary glimpse of its razor sharp teeth before it clamps on your jugular."

"You could take it. Swing your massive purse and pummel it mid-flight. It's dual-action. Club or shield."

I rest my forehead against the cabinet as a wave of exhaustion passes through me. "What's wrong with me, Mark? Why do I do things like this?"

"Cheer up, Cordy, it's not the most impulsive thing you've ever done. What about pledge week in Kristy's jeep when Stacy's grandad pulled you over for suspected intoxication?"

"Omigosh Mark, how did you hear about that?" My head pops up and I look around even though I know I'm alone. "You know I was completely sober, as was everyone else in the jeep," I whisper-yell. "That was—" Math hurts my brain. I rinse my rag as I think. I'm twenty-eight, graduated six years ago, four years at college. Oh, duh. "—ten years ago, and I never told a soul. It was not impulsive. That was pledge week. Had to." Finished with this section, I scoot all the way down the counter.

"Rude." Mark is fully awake now. "I, for a fact, have a soul, and you, for a fact, told me about it. And you never *have* to do anything. There's always a choice. Like signing this lease. You did that all on your own."

I have no memory of telling Mark about pledge week. Sure, I remember the incident in the jeep. We were supposed to drive the loop three times blaring Relient K's "Sadie Hawkins Dance" while only wearing our bras and panties and then we'd get our clothes back, but we were laughing so hard that I was pulled over for drinking *even though I wasn't*. I thought Stacy was going to melt into a flaming puddle of embarrassment in the back seat when the lights flashed behind us.

Sheriff Bellinger must have seen this stunt during pledge week before because he vaulted away from my window with a scowl and a warning to "be careful and quit messing around." He followed us back to campus to make sure of it. Oh, the good old days... but *this* mess...

Sneezing once, I teeter on the edge of the counter and grab the cabinet door for support. It creaks against my weight. I should have waited. I *should* have waited!

Blehhh, I could have at least looked at the place before signing papers.

Who even does that? Oh, yep. *Me*. I'm the problem. I raise my hand in the dingy kitchen while the chorus from Taylor's ever-present song bursts from my lips.

"Did you forget I was still here?" Mark's deadpan voice washes over me.

"Uhhh, yep. You can join me. I'm a free jukebox. What's your pick?"

He groans. "You were quiet for literally five seconds, sneezed, and then started singing. How did you forget I was here?"

"Marky Marky Mark. You're like my little Jiminy Cricket. How'm I supposed to remember every tiny detail of when you're truly there or just skipping through my head in our complex and beautiful relationship?"

He hums "Think of Me" from *The Phantom of the Opera*.

I hold my breath to avoid gagging on droplets of soapy water and vinegar from my spray bottle. I want to tell him about Gilbert Conner. Would it jinx everything if I said it out loud? He might make fun of me. No doubt, Mark would find terrible ways to torture me. In this, I'd like to keep my dreams to myself. He's still humming when I interrupt.

"You should relocate to Nebraska. We would be the best roomies."

"I'll see you in two weeks for Christmas."

"Yeah, but after that it's just me and *the beast* for a year. I'm trembling just thinking of it." The lights pulse when the space heater kicks on.

"Are you climbing the counters to reach the top shelf?"

"Need you ask?"

"That's why you're trembling."

"I don't even know what I'm going to eat for breakfast, and I sign a *twelve month lease with a beast*."

"As your cousin and friend, I demand that you take precautions. Buy yourself a step-stool for Pete's sake."

I have one in the backseat of my car, but this information is none of his business. "You should use that in one of your books. 'A lease with a beast.' It's catchy."

He seems distracted tonight. Normally he'd be halfway into the lecture about how he doesn't write the books but "shreds them to pieces" and doesn't care how authors cry because it's "not my job to hand out cookies."

I love Mark. Even when he's an unyielding boulder, he's my actual favorite. I should set him up with someone. Hmm, who would be perfect for Mark? Someone tough. Not anyone fun and cute like me. He needs an accountant. A lawyer. Or a doctor. What would Mark even do if he had the chance to kiss someone smarter than him?

Heyo! If I were a cartoon, a lightbulb has just materialized over my head. Dr. Nicole Brader! They already have the same last name which, granted, might be a little weird. And their kids would be out of this world intelligent and probably never make friends. Aunt Cordy will have to take them under her wing and teach them how to be cool. *"Follow my lead, young padawans."*

I squat with a foot on either side of the sink to scrub the window and take a moment to sigh over the sprawling Victorian house where my landlord lives across the massive snow covered yard. The whole place glows from the moonlight reflected in magical sparkles off the frozen landscape. I love how the snow enhances everything in the country. It's not food, but I must get pictures of it. I bet I could frame one looking through this window. Add a lamp post just there.

Add that on the list for tomorrow.

"Hey Marky, did you go back to sleep? Are you frantically searching to see if 'beast lease' has already been done?"

Gilbert left a light on upstairs. Is it possible he's still awake at this hour? He probably forgot to switch it off before he went to bed. After all, he left the party early—something a responsible working adult would do. A trail of footsteps through the new snow from his mansion to the side of my hovel catches my attention. Mr. Landlord must have been here recently. Maybe he felt the need to oil the butcher block counters and turn on the space heater. Good for him, but he forgot literally everything else that might need attention.

"Cordy, what d'you need?" Mark leaks his first honest sign of impatience with a sigh. "You do realize I'm in bed. Some of us are required to go into an office for work."

I shove a lock of my wayward hair into the scrunchie that restrains the mess. "Next time don't answer the phone if you don't want to talk."

"So talk. Tell me about your cottage. It's a little dirty? What's really going on? You don't need to call me about a cleaning sesh."

"Well, it's cute at first until you open the cupboards and they stick, and the only heat comes from a box in the corner, and the only excuse for a shower is a copper pipe sticking out of the wall above a corner drain in the bathroom floor. Why wasn't that mentioned? *Hmmm?* I want to like this place, but I feel tricked." I think my feet have gone numb from how long I've been squatting to stare out the window. "Like I've made a huge mistake."

"I'll find him and let him know. File a complaint. Contact the authorities. What's your landlord's name?"

"Miiister Conner." Activate evasive maneuvers! I frantically scrub random things. "He has some explaining to do."

And Aunt Jewels for recommending this place. And Dr. Brader for dangling the papers in front of my nose. I grimace, knowing the fault is my own for snatching it like this was the only chance I'd ever have to affordably live on my own. I'm telling you, the price was *fiiine*. Was I really that desperate to avoid the stomach bug?

"You didn't do any background checks?"

"Puh-lease, Mark. I'm in Hadley Springs, not Omaha or Phoenix. How rude can you be? Background checking a landlord. Psh." I grab my dry rag and polish the window. An unbidden smile lights my face at the way it gleams. Pictures through this window tomorrow will be divine.

"Well, you can always back out and lose your deposit. How bad is it really? Besides the shower?" A yawn slurs his words. I should let him sleep, but I think maybe I'm scared to be alone. "What's his first name?"

"I don't want to tell you because you'll make fun of me."

"I probably will."

"It's just a childhood dream of mine—I know it's silly—"

Mark gasps as if it's the last breath he'll ever take on this earth. "Did you find your first Gilbert?" If Mark was here he'd be pointing an accusing finger at me with a devilish gleam in his eyes. "Oh, Cordy—"

"It's CJ. I'm serious now, remember?"

"Ha! CJ my butt. You locked yourself into a twelve-month lease to fulfill your ridiculous Gilbert fantasies!"

"I did not." I definitely did. "And you can't prove it."

CORDELIA

JOHN WILLIAMS—THE HOUSE, HOME ALONE (ORIGINAL
MOTION PICTURE SOUNDTRACK)

I jump from the counter and land awkwardly on tingling,
blood starved feet. To prevent breaking my ankle, I let it
give and collapse to my hands and knees on the hardwood
floor, dropping my rag and spray bottle and rolling into the
stack of boxes. They teeter, and I curl into a little ball to
protect my face despite my impending death.

*Food Photographer in Beastly Cottage Found Dead
Beneath Crate of Cast Iron Skillets.* The title's long for a
news article, but I'd click it.

"Did you fall off the counter?" Mark doesn't sound the
least bit surprised or concerned. Some friend he is.

"Shh, I jumped," I whisper.

"Why must I be quiet?"

"Boxes are teetering."

"Then move?"

The precarious tower stills, and I release my breath in a

noisy rush. The hot air from the space heater warms my legs, so I sprawl like a starfish basking in a tropical breeze.

"Don't wiggle out of this interrogation, *CJ*. Tell me straight. Do you have designs on the landlord because his name happens to be that of your childhood crush?"

Maybe I do and maybe I don't, but my real issue here is much deeper than my childhood crush on Gilbert Blythe. "Mark?"

"What?" I hear clicks from his pen. That means before he came to his latest Gilbert revelation, *which is utterly false*, he was preparing to ignore me while he completed a few more pages of work. He's probably holding his hand by his ear, pen fisted, thumb clicking while he decides how much red ink he's going to inject into his client's page. He's old-school like that and still prints what he can.

"I'm not going to make my deadline."

The clicking stops. "So help me, Cordy." Mark's held me together for years. At least since Diana left home for college. He's the bow on my shoe. The wind in my sails. The icing on my donut. He does not accept failure as an option.

Hands over my face, I hide from my cousin two thousand miles away. Ten thousand miles. I don't know. However far Arizona is from Nebraska. Forever, that's how far. He's disappointed. As he should be.

There are no proper excuses for my upcoming failure. I have no husband, no kids to pull on my time. Nothing to show for this laziness. Absolutely no reason to be this far behind on work. It's all me. I hear Mark's irritation shouting through his silence. It's in the quiet way he takes a breath, like he's collecting his strength.

"Cordelia Thompson, get off the floor. Go to bed. It's...

geez, one thirty up there?" Blankets rustle on his end. "Are you listening?"

"Mhmm."

"The moment you wake up tomorrow, unpack your camera. Cook the food. Take the pictures. Cook the food and take the pictures!" His voice takes on an edge as if he's lecturing a rebellious teenager. "You're going to finish on time, or your boss isn't going to give you the Easter cookbook. You've already done an insane amount of work to pitch that one. It will be wasted, and you'll have to query all over again. You know this. Get. It. Done." The clicking starts again, angry agitated clicking, and he huffs. Papers shuffle.

I don't even want the Easter cookbook.

Yes, it's good money. My publisher is fantastic. They seem to love me and my work. They would most likely still work with me if I missed some deadlines. But with each contract I die a little on the inside. I want to write stories that matter.

"Mark?"

"You know I'm right here. You don't have to keep saying my name like there's someone else I might think you're talking to. Man, you're annoying sometimes, you know that?"

"Yeah..." I pull myself from the floor and heft an old milk crate to my glossy countertop.

"Sorry, that was a jerk thing to say. You're not annoying."

"It's fine. Someday, I'll marry my dream Gilbert and I won't be in your ear all the time."

He snorts. "Sure thing, Anne-girl."

"When did I tell you about pledge week?" I leave my ten-inch skillet on the gas range and carefully stack the other three in a lower cabinet to the right of the stove. I grip the edge of the counter and work the muscles in my arms and back. My head falls between my outstretched arms, my back flat as an extension of the countertop, and I dig into the warm stretch in my calves. Oh, it feels good. I packed and ran up and down stairs in my shared apartment all morning before the drive.

"Hmm... pledge week. You spilled it during one of our movie-phone nights when I was working in Chicago. *The American President* I think."

"Eww, I did not like that movie." I stand and rip the tape from the top of the next box. Stainless steel pans. "Who even picked that one? Worst choice. Boring, dumb movie. No wonder I fessed all my secrets."

All I hear is the obnoxious clicking in my ears. "Mark, you can hang up, I have more boxes to lug around anyway. My car is still packed with my life."

"You're not going to bed, are you? If I leave you, you're going to open a bag of Cheetos and stand in the corner wondering what to do with your life."

I laugh. My cousin knows me too well. "I won't! I promise."

"Are you out of Cheetos?"

"I'm out of everything."

A cold breeze brushes the back of my neck. I turn to open the next box and there's a man standing in my open doorway with his arms crossed.

"Ahghaaa!" I jump, crash my back into the little table, and knock over the chair. My hands fly over my face and chest, not knowing if they should shield or attack.

The man's eyes grow wide, and he steps back. His mouth moves. I can't hear him, because noise-canceling earbuds. The earbuds that Mark is frantically trying to communicate with me through. "Cordy, answer me. What happened? Are you okay? Hey! Why did you scream?"

I flick one out of my ear, shove it in my pocket, and stare at the imposing stranger in my kitchen. Except... he's no stranger. It's the cello man, Aunt Jewels's nephew, my landlord. It's Gilbert Conner in a grungy outfit covered in sawdust.

"Hi." He nods to the door where icy wind rushes through. "I knocked, but I could see you through the window and it was clear you couldn't hear me." He twitches a nervous smile. "Sorry, I live in the big house over there. I asked Nickie to take care of the paperwork."

He doesn't uncross his arms. Maybe because I'm still trying to catch my breath and I probably resemble a baby rabbit cornered by a fox. "Um, yeah. Hi, Cordelia. I'm your landlord I guess. She didn't tell me it was you. Hi, again." A corner of his mouth tips in a sweet smile. "I wouldn't normally come in like this, or ever. I would never walk in on you."

Mark, who'd gone quiet, speaks in a harsh whisper. "Want me to call 9-1-1? You don't have to stay there with a creep for a landlord."

I cover my ear with my hand. "Shhh." I clear my throat. My heartbeat has reduced to a simmer and I fold in the full picture of Gilbert. Leather work boots, military camo pants, thermal shirt layered under a thick red flannel, crossed arms that highlight his large biceps. Wind reddened cheeks with a long day's worth of stubble, hazel green eyes, and a shaggy head of tarnished bronze hair escaping from a black sock cap.

A gust of wind sends shivers through me. "Shut the door. It's freaking cold."

"Yeah, sorry." He stares—right into my soul—and I don't move as he swings the door with his boot heel.

"Hi again, I guess. I'm CJ Thompson."

He looks like he might smile but doesn't. His eyebrows dip, and he nods once. "Gilbert Conner."

I strike *Let's get hitched.* or *Will you be my boyfriend?* from my list of conversation starters. My gut impulse is to fall into my standard princess curtsy in the middle of the kitchen with a hand to my ear.

"Bye, Mark." I fumble with the earbud. In my haste, I drop it and it rolls under the table. While crawling to retrieve it, my mind buzzes with hamsters running their treadmills. Nothing useful comes to mind.

Nice night we're having. No.

Can I be the Anne to your Gilbert? Run screaming for the hills.

Cool boots! Lame.

This cottage isn't what I'd hoped. Whiny.

How long have you lived here? Intrusive and somewhat boring.

What's your favorite color? How old are we? Five?

Hungry? Yes, but I don't have anything to offer. Unless I do. Hmm, what else was in the bag from Aunt Jewels? Oh, but I left it in the car.

Gross, the floor is sticky under here and from this angle I see dried food stains on the table legs.

Gilbert leans to the side and catches my gaze. "Are you... good under there?"

Ah! My fantasy husband materialized in my kitchen in the middle of the night. I was not prepared for this. *Be cool, CJ!* Be cool.

CORDELIA

PENTATONIX—GOD REST YE MERRY GENTLEMEN

"Found it!" I raise my fist with the escaped earbud before exiting my cave-haven. "Haha, good thing you stopped by. I have questions about the bathroom situation." That's right! Real questions.

He follows me the three steps across the kitchen to the bathroom. There's a stacked washer and dryer combination, toilet, small pedestal sink, and the aforementioned pipe in the wall over a drain in the concrete floor.

I step to the side and make room for him to join me in the cramped space.

He still has his arms strangely crossed with one hand gripping his forearm tightly against his chest. It's an odd posture.

"What am I supposed to do with this?" I wave my hand toward the not-a-shower. "There's no curtain or spigot thingy."

"Sorry, I was going to fix that. I got used to it this way and moved on to the kitchen. Go ahead and pick out whatever showerhead you want, and I'll install it. You'll need to order something online and have it shipped here. The hardware store in town won't carry anything for this. Unless you want to drive to the city."

"And you'll take it off my rent?"

He nods.

"And until then?"

He tips his head to the side like an intrigued dog.

"Until then." I speak slowly. "How'm I going to shower?"

"Oh, it works well enough like this." He nods to the valve with a red handle in the tiled wall. "Turn it all the way on for hot water and a bit back. Just over half-way was perfect for me. The water comes out quick, like a hose—so I do a speed wash, rinse, and get out."

"Or what?"

"Or you'll use up all your hot water in two minutes."

"Two!"

He shrugs. "Maybe five? I don't time it. I just know when I'm slow it's unpleasant. Soap on, soap off, or you'll be cold."

Heat slips into my face as I accidentally picture Gilbert in the shower. He might be having the same thoughts I am because he clears his throat and taps his toe against the wall without looking at me.

"And the water splashes all over the place?"

"Pretty much." He shrugs. "I hang the towel on the hook by the door and wipe the walls down every few days. Use the squeegee to dry the floors. It doesn't take much effort."

Huh. That's what the long-handled squeegee in the corner is for. "You've been living here, then?"

He nods.

"Recently?"

He squeezes past me out of the bathroom. There's a hall closet across from us, and he opens the door. Inside is a cello case. "Recently."

"How recently?"

He points into the closet. "A few hours ago. I didn't expect a renter until after the holidays, but Nickie said it was urgent."

I clasp my face between my hands. "Gilbert! I had no idea. I do *not* need to kick you out of your home. Why were you living here when you've got a house next door? Nickie didn't tell me any of this! She and Aunt Jewels went on and on telling me how *perfect* this place was, and how *lucky* I was to get it before anyone else found out about it."

Gilbert presses his lips together. He looks annoyed. With a shake of his head he mutters, "Typical."

"I'm confused. Did you not want to rent it? Don't *you* own this place? Why put Nickie in charge if you live here?"

"No, Cordelia—"

"CJ."

"Right, sorry. I thought Diana introduced you as Cordelia?"

"She did, but I go by CJ now."

"As of... recently?"

"Yes. You were saying?"

He draws in a breath. "I needed a renter. I asked Nickie if she'd find someone and she volunteered to handle the paperwork since she's at her office everyday. I'll do any maintenance on the place, and yes, I own it. It's all good. She did what I asked. No problem. I would love to do a walk-through with you. Maybe tomorrow? And you can make a list of things you'd want fixed first." He looks past me into the bathroom. "It's functional, but you'll see what I mean. About Nickie—" He lowers his right arm from his chest and pulls away the flannel. His cream-colored thermal beneath is stained red. "So this happened." He replaces his hand before I see the cause of the fresh stain.

"You're hurt!"

"'Tis but a flesh wound."

"Ooookay. Make all the jokes you want—"

"I left my first-aid kit here." He nods to the shelf above the cello in the closet. "I don't suppose you—" His gaze flicks down my petite frame.

"Psh." I jump but cannot quite reach the white box. "Hold on. I got it." With my hand on the door trim. I jump twice more but only succeed in pushing it to the back of the shelf.

"CJ. Move." His chest bumps my shoulder as he reaches over me to grab the box and easily hands it down to me. A pink smear is left where his hand touched it.

"Thank you." Box in hand, I hustle to the table. "I'm glad I was still awake. What would you have done if I'd been asleep like a regular person?"

"I would've figured it out." He hisses as I help fold up his sleeve. There's a slice about three inches long and gaping open a half inch along the top of his forearm.

"Oh my word, Gilbert, what did you do?" I don't give it more than a cursory glance, or I know it will make me sick.

His face is paler than when he came in. "Shoot. This is worse than I thought." He drops his chin to chest. When he lifts it, his jaws are clenched together. "You think it needs stitches?"

"Definitely." I pat him on the shoulder and spend another moment brushing sawdust from his flannel.

"I don't think it's that deep—"

"It's gaping open!"

"But just the skin. It's not like a bone is sticking out. Will you—help me get it wrapped?"

I'd rather not mess with or look at his arm again. "I'll drive you to the E.R."

He snorts. "We're not going to the E.R."

"Yes, we are. You have to get this looked at tonight."

"I agree. Call Nickie, and she'll see me at the clinic in town."

"You can do that?" I snatch his cap and shake the sawdust into the trash can. His hair is matted to his head. I pull my fingers through his bangs to push it away from his face and replace his cap.

"I—" He blinks.

"Sorry, you were making a mess on the floor." I ease into the chair next to him and pretend he's not staring at me funny. "You can make a call and have the clinic opened for you?"

"I—" He shakes his head as if trying to wake up. "I have to. There's no way I'm paying for the E.R. I may as well ask them to cut off my arm and use it as collateral."

"Nobody wants your arm. A kidney, maybe. An eyeball... some bone marrow. Platelets? I don't think there's much else worth taking if you're still breathing."

He lays a square of gauze over the wound and smiles. "We're not going to the E.R." He digs his phone from his pocket and slaps it on the table. "Hey Google, call Dr. Brader."

I'm amazed. "You can do that? You can... call your doctor at—" I pull my phone from my hoodie. "Two a.m. and wait—" I lower my voice to a whisper. "Are you and Nickie, like, a thing?"

He shushes me and shakes his head as Nickie answers

with a singsong voice. "Good morning, dearest. Is this personal or medical? I'm assuming medical."

"Hi, Nickie." He throws me a glance. "You're on speaker. Cord—CJ is here."

"Hi, CJ! You guys having fun? Couple'a cool kids having a late-night party?"

Gilbert leans forward and clears his throat. "Nickie, I'm sorry to bother you. I've had an accident. I, ah, my arm went through my bedroom window."

I gasp, and he looks at me with a shrug.

"I probably need fifteen stitches. Would you mind if—"

We hear shuffling and keys jingling. "I'll be waiting. Park on the side next to my car and come in the back." She sighs. "Darren hates it when I do this, but he'll get over it."

Gilbert shuts his eyes. "Thanks, Nickie. Tell him I'll play at his wife's birthday for free." The call goes dead, and he turns his gaze to me.

"Who's Darren?"

"Office manager at the clinic. But Nickie is his boss."

"Oh."

He moves to sink and washes his hands. When he turns, dripping water on the floor, I rush to my box of cleaning supplies and hand him a dry rag.

"Thanks." Hands dry, he holds pressure against the gauze on his arm. "Your car or mine?"

"Better take yours. My passenger seat is full." I'd only started unloading boxes from the trunk. My back seat is packed to the ceiling, and the passenger's is stuffed with as much as was safe for visibility.

"I can drive myself if you help me wrap it. I need to keep pressure on it though, or I'm afraid I'll bleed out."

I slide my gaze to him without turning my head. "Funny. What happened to 'it's not so deep'?" The thought of tending a gaping wound immediately makes me queasy. "I'll drive. You keep that red stuff to yourself. *Bleed out.* Good grief. Besides, if she gives you anything, you might need someone to drive you home."

"You're sure?"

"Yep." I almost add *that's what friends are for* except we're not friends. I snort. We're barely acquaintances. "You might need to update your tenant paperwork to include late-night drives to the doctor. It could go both ways in case I need you to return the favor."

"I'll have Nickie draft something. She's really good with the professional lingo."

"I'm a writer." I shrug into my heavy purple coat that makes me look like a ripe plum with my coordinating green hat and gloves, but I don't care. It's snuggly. I pop Gilbert's collar up and tug his cap lower to cover his ears against the cold. When I notice he's staring at me, mouth slightly parted, I realize what I'm doing and drop my hands to my sides. "Professional lingo isn't my niche. Ready?" After I shove my feet into my stiff white snow boots, I open the door. A blast of frigid air yanks the breath from my lungs. Head ducked, I speed walk to his blue truck parked thirty feet away by his side door.

We both dive into the cab and slam the doors at the same time.

"Made it!" He raises his injured arm for a fistbump while still holding the wound with his left hand.

I gently tap his fist with my fluffy green one. "Is it still bleeding?"

"I'm afraid to look." A full scale shiver racks his body.

"Where is your coat?"

"I'm fine, let's go."

"You aren't. What if something happens? The truck

breaks down, and we're stranded, and have to walk to town? You wouldn't make it half a mile in this weather." Arms extended, I model my warm coat and knitted mittens. "I would barely make it. My knees are already knocking. Where's your coat? I'll grab it."

He taps his head against the long window behind us. *Tap, Tap, Tap.* Another shiver wracks his body. "Upstairs in the first bedroom."

"I shall return."

I scurry up the front steps into the house. It's warmer inside but not enough. If it's three degrees outside, it's maybe thirty-five degrees here. I flip the lightswitch, and nothing happens. I'm in a mudroom with a stack of boards lining the wall. I make my way into the main house and skid to a stop in a large room. It smells like a campfire. Moonlight streams from the uncurtained windows and reveals a construction zone. The hardwood floors are covered in sawdust. A makeshift table of boards over a couple of sawhorses holds an assortment of tools. The walls are skeletal with yellow spray foam insulation between the studs. White panels of drywall are stacked against the far wall. Red coals glow from a massive fireplace in the center wall of the house.

I carefully make my way to what was once a grand staircase and follow the light to the first bedroom.

It is not a bedroom. The walls are stripped to studs, as downstairs. The floor has been swept and there's a ladder in the corner with a utility lamp clipped to a rung. A duffle bag sits in the corner next to a wrapped up ball of bedding and a carry-on suitcase. There's a step-stool next to the broken window. A wadded T-shirt plugs the hole that I assume his arm went through.

Coat. Right. On the floor near the duffle bag is a brown

canvas work coat. I grab it and a pair of thick gloves and head downstairs.

Back in the truck I toss Gilbert his coat. "Still with me? You didn't bleed out or turn into a popsicle while I was gone?"

"Still here. Let's go, Champ."

"Huh." I angle toward him and stare a moment while he slips his left arm into his coat, leaving the right pressed against his chest. "Thank you," I say.

"What?"

"Of all the nicknames you could have thrown at me, you didn't pick one having to do with my height, weight, or hair color." A swirl of emotion curls in my stomach. We'll address the state of his house later. There is *no way* he's sleeping in that place tonight.

He stares at me with that same funny look on his face from before.

The key is in the ignition on the steering column. I turn it.

He yelps, "Clutch!" the same moment the truck jerks forward and dies.

I narrowly miss slamming my head against the steering wheel. My heart is in my throat, and I'm prickly hot all over with a burst of adrenaline. Slowly, I turn my head to Gilbert.

He's all smiles and sunshine in this dark, cold night. "Clutch," he says again, like that's supposed to mean something to me. "I usually leave it in gear so I don't forget about the e-brake. Sorry."

I glance at the stick between us and look down at the three pedals at my feet and back at him. *Clutch...* I register what this means, yet still I ask. "Gilbert, please explain why there are three pedals in your truck."

GILBERT

VAN HALEN—JUMP

"Clutch. Brake. Gas. I take it this is new?" I tighten my grip along my forearm. It stings but doesn't hurt so much if I keep it perfectly still. If I forget and flex my hand or fingers, I remember why I almost failed high school anatomy. There are over two-hundred-million muscles connecting everything to everything else and at least twelve dozen of them plus all their nerves pass through the gash in my forearm.

Cordelia stares at me. Desperate. Begging. Pleading. If she were a puppy I'd give her whatever she's asked for. Treats? Yes. Frisbee? Absolutely. The look she's aiming at me has probably slayed more than one man. It says, "I want to burrow into a hole and come back when it's sunny. Please, don't make me do this." She's been killing me since I met her at the party. I want to wrap her up in a fuzzy blanket burrito and promise to protect her and keep her safe.

From everything I'd previously heard from Diana and

Nathan, she's not what I'd pictured. They'd painted her as this crazy, fun, outgoing, sometimes-thoughtless adventure girl. But I'm seeing... fragile. A little sad. Tired? And, no, not two in the morning tired, but deeper.

That settles it. We're definitely doing this. I've taught a handful of people to drive using this truck, and they're always thrilled with themselves afterward. I decide she needs this boost. "This will be fun."

She's shaking her head as if that will convince her of some hidden answer to this riddle. "This is a stick shift... a manual?"

Holy moly, this girl is cute. "What shoes are you wearing?" I take in her clunky white snow boots. "Not the best choice for your first lesson."

"There are special shoes for driving a manual?" Her voice rises, and her head still shakes from side to side. Yeah, I could drive myself. The three minutes to Nickie's clinic wouldn't kill me... but this is going to be way more entertaining. Everyone should learn to drive stick at some point.

I scoot closer on the bench seat. "Softer shoes would help you feel the bite, but we'll work with what we've got."

Our breath fogs the air with each exhale. I'm grateful she grabbed my gloves, and I pull them on, sucking air when I flex my right hand, before I lose all feeling in my fingers. She's still shaking her head and now grips the steering wheel with both hands.

"Don't panic. I'm a good teacher."

"This is dumb. You'd better drive—"

"Push the clutch—the one on your left—all the way to the ground."

There goes the head shaking again.

I chuckle. "Yes, go ahead. Nothing will happen."

Her toe can barely tap the pedal. I help her find the bar

under her seat, and she moves it all the way forward. Again she tries the clutch and is able to push it to the floor. "Gilbert, this is *dumb*. This is not the time for a stupid driving lesson."

"Diana told me you were the fun one. She shared a picture of you last year when you jumped out of a plane." I raise my voice to a falsetto. "'Look how much fun Cordy is!' Even Nate's impressed by your independence, but you're telling me you're too scared to learn how to drive stick?"

"Do *not* try to manipulate me!" She's fierce when she turns that stare on me. Puppy turned hawk real fast. It lasts only half a second before a wave of vulnerability washes over her. "*Nathan* said he's impressed?"

"Well, yeah. He wasn't weird or anything, it's not like he talks about you all the time, but sure, I've heard things. Your sister was worried about you that time you were backpacking in France and Nate told her that—let's see, his exact words to Diana were, 'Cordy can take care of herself. It wouldn't surprise me if she comes home married to a French chef wrapped around her baby finger.'"

She scoffs. "I was still with Shaun during that trip. That's just like Nathan to think I'd cheat on my boyfriend."

"Woah." There's some definite fire directed at her brother-in-law. "Point is, you jumped out of a plane. You're going to learn how to drive this truck. Let's go. Clutch down. Break down. Turn the key."

A breath of determination whooshes from her lips. "Cordelia jumps out of planes. I can drive this truck."

"Attagirl."

"Put on your seatbelt." She smiles, and I comply. The engine hums to life. "Now what?"

The headlights spear into white nothingness at the edge of my property. "This is the fun part." I add pressure to my arm. "You'll take your foot off the brake. It shouldn't go anywhere—"

"Shouldn't?! Not like last time when we almost died?"

"It shouldn't *roll* forward because we're not on a hill. Remove your foot from the brake and rest it on the gas. As you feed the gas, slowly release the clutch. Balance the scales."

The engine hums higher as she puts pressure on the gas, and we *lurch* ahead. She squeals and must have lost the clutch because she kills it again.

Pain shoots along my arm. "It's okay." I smile and speak calmly. The main reason I'm a good teacher is because I make a point not to yell at anybody while they're driving. Maybe we could do this tomorrow, but I want this win for her. The roads will be completely empty. The middle of the night really is the best time. The dejection on her face has me offering encouragement. "Do it again. Keep the gas on and go for it. You're not going to hit anything. This time try to feel what the truck's saying. If it's going, then go."

"Um, your truck is saying, 'It's two in the morning, *dumb-dumb*. Your landlord is a bleeding *moron* and you should take your own car.'" Her fists pound a tantrum against the steering wheel. "Crap! We can't even take my car!"

She looks at me with those large eyes laced with panic. "The gas light came on before I got into town and then I drove all the way out here. No, we're good. I probably have another five miles in her, except—" A shuddering breath breaks the last of her spirit. "I left the trunk open again, didn't I? No! Don't even look. Quit it! Eyes forward. I know what I did. Why do I always do that?"

Her gesturing hands move as fast as her words. "I always

leave it open because I'm coming right back out. But do I ever remember to go back out? No, I don't. There's always something, isn't there? This time it was your filthy cabinets." She shoves a mittened finger at my nose. "I left the trunk open, and that means the battery is dead." Her head falls back, and she fake cries. "Boo-hoo-hoo." Wow. Is she always this dramatic or only in the middle of the night? "And now I have to drive your stupid truck before you bleed to death because you punched your arm through a window."

"I won't bleed to—"

"Lands to the living, Gilbert!"

"Lands to the what?"

"Why didn't you go to bed like you were supposed to? *Hmmm?* Oh, that's right, because *you* don't have a bed. So instead, you're up on a ladder in the middle of the night? Next to a window? This is insane. Insane! And no, it isn't at all the same as me climbing the countertops, so don't even bring it up. I had to do that because your cottage is filthy. But you living in that house right now is ridiculous. I can't believe you did that. You can't sleep there." She blows out three successive breaths as if she's about to go underwater and holds the last one.

Clutch. Brake. Ignition.

And we're off again. We still jump forward, but she manages to keep the gas down. We loop around the cottage through the few inches of snow in the yard and careen down the driveway. She slows at the turn for the highway, but since she doesn't stop entirely, we're okay.

"Cordelia, you're doing great." I speak as I might to an injured animal. Smooth and calm. "We need to shift again. It'll be like when we first started. Take your foot off the gas, and punch the clutch with your left foot." She does, and I shove the gear into second. "Balance the gas as you release the clutch."

We lurch forward, and I involuntarily wince. "This is fine. Let's keep it here."

"At... eighteen miles an hour?"

"Yes."

She sits ramrod straight, expression grim.

"You doing okay?"

"You called me Cordelia again. Earlier. My name is CJ."

I don't buy it. She called herself Cordelia not two minutes ago. CJ doesn't fit her at all. "Does it bother you that much? Nate always referred to you as Cordelia or Cordy, so that's what I have in my head."

"He's never mentioned you."

"Ouch." I don't miss that she avoided the question.

She clicks her tongue. "Sorry. That was rude—"

"I'm messin' with you. You're an interesting person, and it's obvious they're proud of you. It would be weird for them to talk about me. We're not super close or anything. We both attend the men's Tuesday Bible study. We see each other at church and my aunt's parties."

The engine whines a little too high. "Slow down unless you're ready to try shifting again. We'll be into town in a minute."

"I'm afraid I'll break your truck."

"He can handle it."

"Clutch. Shift. Gas?"

"Ready... go!"

She shakes her head.

So we stay at fifteen miles per hour. The gravel road packed with snow transitions to blacktop. The headlights bounce from a pile of snow on the shoulder. There are no stars through the overcast sky that speaks of new snow on its way.

"I don't know where to go from here."

"Turn right on seventh. Go ahead and slow down." I glance at her tense face. "You'll need to downshift. Think you can manage it?"

"No! I don't even know what that stick thingy does."

"Gear shift." I laugh under my breath. "Stick thingy works."

"I haven't touched it."

I am usually a much better teacher. It's now two twenty-eight as the square green lights on the dash remind me. Maybe that has something to do with it. I forgot to give her the opening instructions, the layout of the gear shift, what to do for turning and stopping. What's gotten into me? Too late now.

I help her down shift, but she stalls going around the corner and kills the engine. The next three blocks through town are a joke. She stalls two more times.

"Quit laughing at me," she says while laughing. "We're going to get the cops called on us, and I will blame you. I don't even have my license with me. Oh my gosh, can I get a ticket for that? Sure, you think that's real funny." Her fuzzy mittened hand slaps my chest. "Make fun all you want, but I will drag you to jail with me, and you'll never get your arm sewed back together."

"I'm not making fun of you. You're just really cute when you get all flustered."

She gasps. "I am not cute!"

The way she yells this as if her threatening voice will have any effect has me laughing more than I have the whole drive so far.

"Gilbert, pay attention. There's another stop sign. I'm not stopping. I'm not stopping!"

"You're good. Go, go, go!" We roll through town at nine miles per hour as she freaks out. "There is nobody out here. That's the clinic on the left."

We see Nickie's red Honda. "Clutch. CJ, clutch!" She does, and we jerk to a stop when she punches the brake too. We've successfully double-parked, and the engine's still running.

Cordelia claps her hands and graces me with an excited smile. "I did it! Now what?"

I shift into reverse. "Turn off the engine."

She does and then slumps into the seat. "That was awful but really cool. When you're not bleeding to death, and it's sunny, and the roads aren't covered in snow, will you teach me for reals?"

I nod. "Sounds like a date."

Her eyes grow like a chia commercial.

"Not a date date. A plan. That's a good plan. I don't date. I'm not—" Wow, she wears every one of her emotions on her face. She's a charcuterie board of feelings and I think she's moved along the scale from complete shock at the suggestion of a date with me to absolute despondency when I dismiss the idea. "What I'm saying is I think you should learn how to drive a manual, and I have the truck and live conveniently nearby, and I'm usually a great teacher. That's what friends are for, right?"

And for dessert we have awestruck hope. She tugs her hat on the sides. "We're friends?"

"Cord—" My gaze flits from her mittens pulling the green hat, the freckles dotting her cheeks, the little crease along her forehead that speaks more than her words. I take in her soft, expectant words and offer a half-smile. "CJ, anyone who drives me to the doctor in the middle of the night is my friend. Thank you. I'm going to get my arm poked with a few needles now. You might want to come inside where it's warm."

She unbuckles her belt, and then mine, and then she's all up in my space. My lungs freeze as she leans across me to open my door. Oh. That was... thoughtful. And not remotely disappointing.

CORDELIA

JOHN DEBNEY—MAIN TITLE, ELF (ORIGINAL MOTION PICTURE SOUNDTRACK)

"I almost gave up on you." Nickie holds the door for us. "But I see you've added another name to your list?"

Gilbert winks at me over his shoulder. "Almost. She'll need a few more lessons."

Nickie walks alongside me as we follow Gilbert down a thin carpeted hallway. "Hi, CJ. Didn't expect to see you again so soon."

I jerk my chin toward the broad back before us. "I'm sure he could've driven himself, but I was still up."

"You two deserve each other then."

Gilbert coughs. "And here we are." With jaw clenched, he sends Nickie a *knock-it-off* glare.

Undeterred, she pats his chest as she glides past him through the doorway. "You know the drill, sir." Nickie rolls over a cart with a tray of doctory-looking things. "Sit."

I hesitate in the hall. "Um. I think I'll... find something else to do."

"Come in, girl." She points to a chair across the room. "Turn that one around, and we'll chat."

"Ope, it's fine, really—"

"Sit."

I huff and fall into the pleather chair with wooden arms. It's large for my size. I easily slip my feet free of their boots and curl my legs under me. A stack of *Good Housekeeping* and *Nebraska Farmer* is spread out on the side table.

I do everything I can to ignore what's happening on the other side of the room. And as much as Nickie invited me to chat, she and Gilbert are having their own fervent and hushed conversation. Awesome. They're bickering like— well, either siblings or lovers.

During our drive I never asked for more details about their relationship. Pretty convenient to be besties with a doctor. "How does this work?"

They fall silent and look at me.

Too late, I turn away after noticing a red splotch on Nickie's blue glove.

"This." I stare at the wall and wave my hand around the room. "Is this like a friends and family discount thing? How many are gutsy enough to ask you to open your own clinic after hours instead of driving to the E.R.?"

"Gilbert Conner." Nickie breathes out a laugh. "My darling Gil is the only one. I'd do it for my brother John, but he, unlike some men I know, never requires my services."

Gilbert snorts, and she narrows her eyes. My face heats at the rude double meaning.

"John, the piano player?" I've closed my eyes because I really do *not* care to see any needles or more evidence of the wound.

"Yep," Nickie says. "He and Gil have been creating art of some kind since—" She hums. "Fifth grade?"

"At least. Remember the comic strip? That was with Mrs. Torres in third."

"You can call her Marie now."

"I don't think I can. Mmmrs. Torres. See?"

They go on like this for another ten minutes, and a little part of me—correction—a big part of me, wishes I shared these memories. Gilbert and Nickie are intimately connected. Known each other since elementary school. Same circle of friends. Church, school, small-town life. Best friend's big sister. Gilbert was probably in and out of her house like it was his own.

"Did you two ever date?"

Silence.

My bad. Was that an awkward question? I chew my lower lip and peek at them. Gilbert and Nickie gaze at each other, not me. *Shoooot*. What can of beans did I open?

Gilbert gives a side smile. "Yeah, we tried that once."

"It didn't work out." Nickie squints at Gilbert and shakes her head.

"Sorry, that was none of my business." And I wish I had kept my mouth shut. "You guys just seem really close, so I wondered. But yeah, sorry, that wasn't my place to ask. Sometimes I say things—"

"It's fine, Cordelia." He shrugs. "It was a long time ago. Wow." He chuckles and shifts his gaze back to Nickie, whose head is bent over his arm. "Twelve years ago?"

She whistles low. "Senior prom."

I picture her in a puffy yellow princess dress with her blonde hair in an updo with curled tendrils along the side of her face. Or maybe a midnight blue slinky gown with rhinestones. A yawn to beat all yawns hits me from nowhere. Of course, I crash *now*.

Nickie rips off one of her gloves. "All done. Keep it clean. Remove the sutures in ten days or so."

"Thanks, Nickie."

"Yep, you've done me a favor, but I didn't want to inflate your ego. I'm on call tonight for the E.R. so I would've been your girl either way. But now I get a free ticket!"

She gathers the soiled gauze and dumps it in the trash before addressing me. "Gil always pays me with a date to the Lied Center whenever a Broadway show comes through. You should join us next time. I almost thought I'd have to take myself this year."

Gilbert stands. "She exaggerates. This is only the third time she's opened the clinic for my sake." They exchange a fond glance that feels too private for me.

My heart sinks. I want *that*. Oh, don't be silly. I'm not pining after Gilbert Conner. I just... I don't know. I want the easy connection. Layers of trust that only come with time. Where's my two a.m. friend? I never would have called Shaun after eleven.

There's always cousin Mark, I suppose. But I wonder if he sees me that way. He loves and supports me. Would Mark call if he needed anything in the middle of the night? Who am I kidding... Mark never needs anything. He's way too put together. Gilbert though, he seems like someone I'd get along with. Although Gilbert came to the cottage for the first-aid kit, not for *me*.

Gilbert says we're friends now—or could be? There may not be room for me in this town where everyone already fits into the puzzle.

Nickie grabs a bottle of disinfectant and washes the seat he's just vacated. I wrap my arms tighter around my legs and drop my head to my knees.

Clue in, CJ. By all appearances, Gilbert's a great guy,

but I know the only reason I'm here is because I was the closest creature with a driver's license. If my kitchen light had been off, he'd never have disturbed me. He didn't even know it was me in the house until he walked in. Since I surely don't want to play the lead in a cheesy Christmas movie, I need to get over this childish crush pronto. It takes more than a chance encounter at one party for two people to fall in love.

Fall in love. Yuck.

I don't want to fall in love—I want to be immersed in it. Is it possible to be so accepted that I'm never scared to be fully me? It ain't a thing.

My rebranding will work. I can do better. CJ can be more serious and focused.

Starting after my next full night of sleep.

My breathing slows. The swish of Nickie's rag on the vinyl further relaxes me. Calling Mark instead of going to bed wasn't very on-brand for CJ.

It shouldn't be so hard to be alone. I wasn't scared this evening or anything so mundane. There was no premeditated reasoning. Because I had all the thoughts and all the feelings and I was alone with them, I called Mark.

When I decided to look for a place to rent, I was excited for the chance to have a place all to myself. I didn't realize I lacked the common sense required to do life.

Tomorrow, I'll do better. Gilbert probably thinks I'm incredibly immature to be up this late polishing a kitchen instead of sleeping. He'd be right.

A hand falls to my shoulder and wakes me from a half-sleep.

"Come on, Champ." Gilbert's grip tightens then disappears as I raise my head. "I'll drive us home." He works to pull his hat over his head with one hand.

I can't handle the awkwardness of his one-handed struggle, so I snatch it away and do it for him. He lets me help without a fuss though he bites the tip of his tongue on the side of his mouth and crinkles his nose.

"Quit it." I try not to giggle at his expression. "Let's go home." My eyes widen at my words and I speed walk down the hall before anything else slips out.

CORDELIA

FRANK SINATRA—LET IT SNOW

"I'm not sleeping in your bed." Gilbert holds the front door of the cottage and waves for me to walk in first. Blessed warm air welcomes us into the kitchen.

"It's not my bed." I stomp my snowy boots past him. "I don't care if I signed the papers. If you're so small-town friendly that you can call a doctor to stitch you back together in the middle of the night in exchange for *show tickets*, you can sleep in *your* bed—"

"Except it's no longer my bed!" He waits by the front door, no longer smiling.

I figured he wouldn't willingly agree to this, so I *might* have tricked him into coming inside by asking him to carry my large duffle while I juggled a black trash bag stuffed with a few pillows and blankets.

I lead the way through the dine-in kitchen, past the bathroom across from the closet, and into the bedroom. An old-fashioned four-poster bed with a bare mattress sits in the middle of the room. There's a closet on one side, a dresser on the other.

Gilbert halts outside the bedroom, my bag slung over his shoulder with two fingers like it's nothing. "And where will you sleep?"

"The floor's fine."

"You're not making sense. It's okay for you to sleep on the floor and not me?" He examines the room. "I have bedding on the floor of my own room."

I shudder from the lingering cold. "It is not livable in that house. Do not speak to me of your bedroom. *Olaf* wouldn't be comfortable in that house."

He cuts his gaze to me before he mutters, "I have a fireplace."

I stomp my foot on the hardwood floor and release a childish scream. Gilbert's eyebrows jump. He's about to laugh at me again. Before he has the chance, I spring forward and poke my mitten covered finger into his cheek. "You're not taking this seriously."

He slowly pushes my duffle into my chest, and I step back. And back and back as he advances. I refuse to take the bag, and he raises an eyebrow.

"Here's what's going to happen, CJ. You're going to lie down. I'm going to the big house. And we're both going to sleep in our separate rooms."

My thighs bump the edge of the bed, and I angle to the side to avoid being pushed over. "I won't be able to sleep because I'll be picturing your cold, lifeless form turned blue after the shivers finish wracking your body and your heart locks up because your blood turned into a cherry slushie." I pivot around Gilbert, and now his back is to the bed. With enough force that my boot skids on the floor, I shove against the bag he's still holding. "Just say no to hypothermia."

He plops on the mattress—by choice, not because I was strong enough to make him. "You're that worried?"

"It's not camping weather, Gilbert! Look it up." I jut my hip out and cross my arms.

With arms resting on the bag on his lap, he unlocks his phone. His shoulders slump and he drags a hand down his face. "Fifteen below and dropping. Windchill negative forty-five."

Hello, Nebraska! You'd think that would be enough to convince anyone. But he purses his lips and stares through me in deep thought. What is with this determined show of chivalry? It's four in the morning, dude. Go to sleep already.

I unzip my puffy purple coat. "Are you afraid I'll bother you during the night?"

He chuckles. "I'm sure I could fend you off. No, I just—"

Dipped eyebrows and a sigh express his deep anguish.

"Just like that?" I noisily suck a lungful of air to add to his theatrics. "So confident! For all you know, I have a black belt in Kung Fu Karate." My hands slice the air in a very convincing demonstration.

"Well." His expression softens into a tired smile. "Now we all know you're full of lies and have never trained a day in your life."

"Tae Kwon Do?" I pause after a sidekick and turn my head to face him.

"Pick one." He stifles a yawn. "Maybe you meant Tai Chi or Jiu-jitsu?"

"All of them." I wave my hands erratically. "The fighting with the martial arts! I have a black belt in taking down tough guys. I break boards with my head."

"Okay, sure. You're a mighty warrior. I'm convinced."

"Good. So you know I can take care of myself if

anyone tries something." With an expressive show of strength, I grab the trash bag with my bedding and rip it open with my bare hands. Working quickly, because he's sitting on the bed and this is the only chance I'll get, I toss my pillow at the head of the mattress and push my finger against the brown canvas of his coat. He holds against the pressure.

For the first time since we've met, I don't have to tip my head to look up into his eyes. His gaze holds mine, and I don't know what he's thinking. It could be, "How soon can we order a pizza?" or "Is there a different path Alice should have taken through the Tulgey Wood that would have bypassed the Mad Hatter's tea party?"

Oh, please. The only crazy person thinking those thoughts is me—and I already know there's no place in town that delivers pizza. Pity, that.

He finds his answers or gives up because he slumps sideways onto the pillow. A quiet groan escapes, and a grin spreads across his face with his eyes closed. "I'm afraid. I'd better go to my own house to be safe."

"Shh. Rest for a minute, then you can go freeze if you really want to."

In a matter of seconds his breathing grows heavy, and his face relaxes. Boots on the floor, coat zipped to his chin, and injured arm slung over my duffle bag like a teddy bear, he's asleep. I'm not surprised. Give me three seconds with my eyes closed, and I'll be there. I've officially been awake for twenty-three hours.

Good. Grief.

I roll the fancy heater box into the bedroom and make use of the bathroom. I remember to turn off my phone to ensure I won't have any alarms going off in an hour. A notification for nine unread messages snags my attention.

Mark: Are you okay?

Mark: Please tell me you're sleeping and not kidnapped.

Mark: Hey! ARE YOU ALIVE?

Mark: I'm glad you called and got me riled up before you went missing. This is going to be awful when I'm the last witness and should have called the cops. With my luck, they won't start a search until you've been gone for 24hrs.

Mark: I'm going back to bed. Please tell me you're not dead.

Mark: Turning off the light. If there's no message from you when I wake up I'm calling the police and Diana.

Mark: In that order.

Mark: Good night. If you're not in a ditch somewhere.

Mark: And then I'll call your mom and probably my mom.

Cordelia: All is well. Thanks for checking on me. I'll call you tomorrow.

Cordelia: I had an interesting night. I learned to drive a stick shift! Sort of. I'm not very good at it yet. Turning off my phone.

Back in the bedroom, Gilbert has pulled his feet, still in his boots, up on the bare mattress. He's sleeping on the very edge, and the other half beckons me. And I really *really* want to be asleep. And I want to sleep for a very *very* long time.

I turn off the light.

And, yeah. I climb into bed next to a man I met a few hours ago.

I toss my quilt over him and wrap myself in a thick fleece blanket with little snowmen dancing with elves. I'd say that I fell asleep before my head hit the pillow—but no, it's at least a few seconds later because there's enough time for me to notice the sound of the wind against the little house. It's a desperate, agitated sound.

I snuggle deeper into my second favorite pillow. The wind can do what it wants tonight because I'm not out there. I'm here. In my new cottage. Safe and sound with my stitched-up, cello-playing landlord friend.

12

CORDELIA

JOHNNY CASH—THAT CHRISTMASY FEELING

A door clicks shut and I pop open my eyes. No screaming wind. No alarm. And no soft breathing across the bed. But there are suspicious smells. Good smells. Delightful smells. Fresh coffee smells.

My quilt is rumpled at the foot of the bed and there's an imprint in the pillow beside me. Proof last night wasn't my imagination. I have no idea of the time, but sunshine pours through the dusty green curtains on both windows. A muted engine rumble clues me into Gilbert's whereabouts.

I arch like the queen of all cats and slide myself off the bed. The moment my toes reach the cold wood, I fall into a wide-legged stance and windmill my arms to the floor, around, and up to the ceiling in a good-morning stretch.

Oh! No wonder the coffee smell is so strong. On the dresser sits a little tray with a paper bag advertising a donut shop and a French press of liquid happiness next to a clear glass mug. An oddly familiar mug that I packed in a box yesterday morning. I take a step closer and notice a folded scrap of paper with my initials.

CJ,

Thanks for the late-night adventures. Holler when you're ready for another driving lesson. You did great.
GH

A warm shiver zings through to my toes and I bite my lower lip to suppress a giggle. I did *not* do great. I managed to get us to town. Barely.

I carry the whole tray into the kitchen to look for cream, but there's not a clear surface in sight. All my things that I'd left in the car have magically transferred themselves to cover every inch of the kitchen. How I had all of this crammed into my car is a mystery to all but the vehicle itself. But here it is. A box marked "Summer" sits beside another marked "Current Project" and "Unpack First."

After I balance the tray on the corner of a laundry basket filled with my shoes, I'm pleasantly surprised to find cream in the fridge along with a half-empty bottle of ketchup and two sticks of butter. Just the essentials, I see.

From the window above the sink I notice three things right away: Smoke billows from the chimney of the big house, Gilbert's truck is parked at a strange angle next to where my car used to be, and my car is missing.

"What in the world?" I grip the warm mug in both hands.

He managed to go out and buy breakfast, unload all of my possessions, make coffee—with my French press and electric kettle—and steal my car while I slept.

Gilbert stole my car!

Even if I know in my heart there must be more to this story, this simply doesn't fit any scenario I imagine.

I check the hall closet for his cello. It's not there.

The emptiness shouldn't hit so personally. I stand in the hallway hugging my mug against my chest and try not to be depressed about a missing cello. This feels significant. He will probably avoid me from now on because I forced him to sleep over. But I had a good reason! We'd both been awake for way too many hours. His house was—is—uninhabitable. How long does it take to build a fire? Heat the room? And then to sleep on a cold, hard floor? That would have been equally foolish.

A sip of my poor man's latte warms my core while I contemplate life. Gilbert is already going about his day. No need to make it a thing.

I wonder how his arm feels.

Gosh, I have so much work to do. This was a dumb week to move across the state. I have most of the recipes photographed, thank goodness, but I've not typed the blurb for any of them and I need to put together one last spread of holiday pies. Running away to Hadley Springs this week was a terrible career move. Yes, I can work from anywhere. But I could have held it together for a week until I'd met the current deadline, joined Diana for the holidays as planned, and then moved to town. Classic Cordelia making impulsive life-altering decisions at the drop of a hat. Or drop of a fiancé, as the case may be.

A heavy weight presses against my ribcage that makes breathing a dedicated effort as I stare at the empty closet. I close my eyes and tip my face to the ceiling. My heart has been taking lessons from Bambi's friend, Thumper, and its deep rhythm is almost audible to my high strung nerves. I feel myself spiraling into a pit of overwhelm which often leads to stare-at-the-wall-and-do-nothing for the rest of the day.

No!

I turn on my heel, spilling coffee in the process. No time for this self-doubt. I search for my phone—it's under the bed —and turn it on. I have eight voicemails that I ignore. Poor suckers. One of these days I'll get around to changing the memo: "If you leave a voicemail, I will never listen to it. Please text instead." But today is not that day. Or tomorrow.

It's ten thirty-eight. Past time to get going.

My attempt to shower is an experience. The way the water spits from the pipe in the wall and the cold concrete floor throws me into flashbacks of summer camp and I'm very thankful the walls aren't also covered in June beetles and mayflies.

Clean, dressed, coffeed, and carbed by eleven, I plunk my day book on the edge of the table and frantically brain-dump.

Today: December 15, 11 AM
1. Breathe. You can do hard things.
2. Move bedroom boxes out of kitchen
3. Clean counters, stove top, table
4. Find notes for Christmas Classics: Desserts
5. Eat food
6. Detailed plan to finish WIP by Thursday
7. Shop for ingredients
8. Check on Diana and the plague
9. Text Mark
10. Order showerhead
11. Put sheets on bed
12. Eat more food
13. Draft email to publisher

14. Review/edit outline for Easter cookbook
15. Find Xmas list and order stuff I forgot
16. Call Mom
17. Finish unpacking
18. Set up office in bedroom

My chest tightens when I review the list. On what crazy planet could I possibly do all of this in one afternoon? I stare at number one until the print grows blurry. I flip over the page and scribble the header for tomorrow.

I circle half of today's list and mark them for later. Then I snatch my phone to take care of the easiest one.

> Cordelia: Marky Mark! Busy day. I'm determined to meet my deadline because I'm a freaking boss. Sorry I bothered you last night. Hope you get a nap today.

I cross off number nine.

> Mark: Glad you're alive.

> Cordelia: Why were you so worried? I can take care of myself.

> Mark: I'll ignore that you call in the middle of the night on a weekly basis.

> Cordelia: *GIF of Ash throwing a Pokemon ball with "I choose you!" along the bottom*

> Mark: Get to work. In a meeting, and my boss is throwing me dirty looks.

> Cordelia: Tell him it's a family emergency

> Mark: Her. She'd tell me to clock out and take care of it on my own time. Ciao.

94

Cordelia: Chow.

Before I become distracted by doom scrolling, avoidance research, or randomly texting more friends, I turn my phone off and hide it in the silverware drawer. I punch the air a few times to increase blood flow and decide *today is the day* that I start writing blurbs for this cookbook... after I write a new item on my list.

19: Ask Gilbert to marry me.

Haha. Just kidding. I cross it off. Scribble scribble scribble until the whole line is covered in ink and nobody will ever know that I'm a crazy person.

GILBERT

SURVIVOR—EYE OF THE TIGER

"Pivot! Pivot!" John directs from the stair landing below. He's been yelling random instructions since we hauled the mattress out of his Grandma's upstairs bonus room. I set my end on the toe of my boot and rest my bandaged forearm on the mattress. A strumming pulse of a bass guitar has taken residence in my arm, but it's still wrapped tight from last night—er, this morning—so I'm not worried about pulling stitches.

"Gil! What're you doing?" John's question comes with a laugh before he drops his corner. "I've got thirteen minutes before they send out the dogs. Let's go."

"You don't get the full hour for lunch?"

"Manager training videos. They keep trying to promote me so they can have someone else open and close, and I don't have the heart to turn them down."

"Come with a pay raise?"

"Yeah, but then I'm awarded the curse of inventory. I

hate every minute of inventory. Now, what we really need to do is record—"

"At least it's steady work."

"Steady work at the grocery is great for paying bills." He sighs. "You've got to look at our numbers on the website, and our YouTube channel is on the cusp of going viral. I won't have to stock shelves for long."

John records our practice sessions and has a number of our original songs on file somewhere. Thanks to his work, I gave a CD to Aunt Jewels last year for Christmas. He's got bigger plans though. He wants to schedule regular gigs in the city. He wants to sell our music and get merch and tour coast to coast. John thinks a few uploads to Spotify will have us set for life.

I'm not willing to bet anything on it. I love the shows we've done so far. But when he starts talking about opening for other bands, or following some kind of promotional schedule across multiple states, I don't know what to tell him. What's so wrong with playing at local events, church, and family gatherings? A few weddings here and there, a few events in the surrounding cities. I love writing and playing music. But I don't trust it for a living.

Maybe flipping houses isn't any more reliable than selling my music. For some reason the work with tools and lumber feels more secure. People always need their houses fixed. Music? It's for the dreamers—music could never support a family full-time unless you make it big in a city. I'm not cut out for that kind of life.

I jerk my chin to signal John to pick up his end. "Ready. Up." We haul the double mattress into the bedroom and lean it against the wall.

John whistles in approval. "You've been busy."

More like frenzied. Hectic. Agitated. I popped out of

bed at the cottage after three hours of sleep and haven't stopped moving since.

Sleeping on that bed—her bed—was unacceptable. I don't know what possessed me to lie down. And I never would have done it if I'd thought for a second she was going to cuddle up next to me. Even if she didn't cuddle. She was there, right there, while I slept. Which, maybe isn't so bad, but it sounds bad.

I don't know where I thought she would sleep, but when her face was the first thing I saw upon waking—completely relaxed, peaceful—I felt completely relaxed and peaceful. And I don't like it.

Some far-away day in the distant future, I'll enjoy mornings beside the love of my life. I'll reach over and smooth her hair behind her ear. She'll open her eyes and smile lazily. I'll have those moments with my wife. Relaxed and peaceful moments. I don't want them with a girl I met once at a party.

How could I have let myself stay over? I'm her *landlord*. It doesn't matter if it made sense, that it was dangerously cold, that it was almost morning or that her family is sick with a stomach bug. Sleeping together, even if we weren't *together*, crossed so many boundaries. I don't want to think about it.

Yes, you could say I've been busy today.

I finished hanging the drywall in this room less than an hour ago and now that I have a mattress, there will never *ever* be a repeat of what happened last night. I even sealed the window frame with plastic until I can replace it come spring. It looks terrible, but I'll deal with it in time.

John snaps in my face. "Where'd you go?"

I blink, avert my gaze from the window, and stare at John. "What?"

"Nevermind." He rests against the doorframe and nods to the cottage where my attention has been drawn every few minutes today. "How's CJ? You moved into this huge dump before it's ready—she must have really twisted your finger."

A false laugh escapes. *Nothing to see here. She's not twisted me into doing anything.*

"Nothing like that." I walk my fingers along the bandage under my sleeve in an attempt to ease the burning sensation. "Your sister bushwhacked me. I didn't know who the new tenant was until after papers were signed. And after—" After I introduced myself in the middle of night. "Nevermind."

"After," John says. As if that explains everything. He cocks his head. "You're saying you'd have moved into a shell with no heat or bed regardless. You'd do it for anyone. Not just a red-headed sprite with a contagious smile."

I shake my head. "Don't start. It was Nickie. And with Aunt Jewels shoving every available woman within fifty miles at me, I don't need it from you." I wrestle the lid off the five-gallon bucket of white drywall mud. All this standing around is wasting time. "Toss me that water bottle."

John watches me stir a few ounces of water into the top layer of mud until it's silky smooth while he unrolls a length of paper tape. I spread a layer of mud along the seams of the drywall with my six-inch putty knife, and he follows and presses the tape over the mud.

"If you're not into her..." John fumbles with the roll of tape before extending another length. "Do you mind if I ask her out?"

The surge that crescendos in my gut surprises me. A dollop of mud falls to the floor. Since when does John ask me who he dates? As if I have authority over him. There was Emily in tenth grade that we both liked, but then she never liked either of us.

I turn my back and work the rest of the mud from my knife into another seam. "I'm not dating." I remind myself as I speak it out loud. "You know this. I'm done with women until I sell this house and buy another to flip. Too much needs done for me to take time off to play with girls." I dampen my annoyance. John meant no harm. There shouldn't be such cacophony clouding my thoughts on this topic. "Why are you asking? I don't have feelings for Cordelia. If you want to take her out, be my guest."

"Awesome. Thanks, man."

"Don't thank me. That makes it weird."

I bend to scoop the fallen mud from the floor and see Cordelia standing in the doorway to my bedroom, face flushed. Her green mittens tighten around a gift box covered in red and white striped paper until it bends against the pressure.

I bolt upright. "Hey—Hi."

She greets me with a small smile, and her gaze darts between John and me.

I share a glance with John. What did she hear? All of it? I silently implore him to play it cool.

"Amazing." She recovers faster than either of us. "This room looks completely different than last night."

John narrows his eyes as if catching me in a lie. I almost blurt into the room that Cordelia took me to the hospital and then I slept in her bed.

Cordelia—I'm having a hard time even thinking of her as CJ—sets the box on the floor. "A little housewarming present. To keep you warm." She tucks her hands into the pockets of her oversized purple coat. "I went to town after my car came back."

Her gaze travels around the room and I'm wondering what she truly thinks of my home. My work. This mess.

She nudges the box with her foot. "I went to town for groceries. You wouldn't believe my good luck. Remember how the car was dead because I'd left the trunk open forever?" Her gaze darts around the room, landing on everything but me.. "My car started just fine... it seems a little Christmas elf jumped the battery and put gas in her. You wouldn't happen to know anything about this?"

I lift my gaze to the ceiling. Yes, I jumped her car and filled the tank with gas. But give me a break. She drove me to the clinic in the middle of the night, in a truck she didn't know how to operate, and then insisted I sleep in a warm bed. Taking care of her car was the least I could do. And unloading it, but that was a simple thing. Goodness, yeah, okay, I also brought her donuts and made her coffee.

I know how this looks, but there was a box labeled: "Yummy coffee, unpack first." Therefore, I obliged. I'm pleased she slept through the morning. Hopefully she's recovered from last night.

John pokes his elbow into my side. "Elves, you say?"

"Apparently." I angle the putty knife and the white slop oozes the other way.

Her shoulders rise to her ears as she tunnels her hands into her coat pockets. She looks like she's trying to shrink into her plum coat.

I'm kicking myself for talking about her with John. It wasn't bad... was it? I try to remember exactly what I said. That I didn't know her? Wasn't interested? John could have her? Oh, perfect. Let's barter over the new girl on the market.

Whatever it was, it's enough to make her uncomfortable.

"Listen—" I start.

"John, will you—" she says.

We both stop. This is awkward. It shouldn't be. But it is.

It's not that I'm *un*interested. Let the record state that I do not dislike my new tenant.

How would I feel if I overheard a girl tell her friend that she didn't want to go out with me? Dating her isn't the problem. I'm not dating anyone! If I were, she'd be a great option. But if I'm not dating, then of course I'm not dating *her*.

Crud. Why are the three of us standing around like middle schoolers who suddenly can't talk to their friends because they've just learned how babies are made?

She smiles at John and relaxes her posture. "I know I overheard a conversation that wasn't meant for me."

Wow, she just goes for it. I'm in awe. Good for her. The confidence of this woman astounds me.

"Would you like to grab dinner with me tonight? It's—" She pulls out her phone and checks the time. "—almost four."

"No!" John zips his coat and pats his pockets, probably checking for his phone and wallet. "Sorry, yes! That'd be great. I would love to. I have to get back to work, but I could pick you up at seven fifteen? Is that too late?"

Yes, it's too late. She meant for you to take her out now for an early supper. She was awake all night long—with me, but that's irrelevant—and needs to go to bed early.

Her shoulders rise and fall with a happy sigh.

I raise my eyebrows at the odd feeling her joviality is forced.

"I'm happy to meet you somewhere," she says through a smile. "Is there a place in town we could go? I don't feel like staying up late tonight."

See? Told you.

John makes a face like he's smelled something gross. "Subway or gas-station pizza. You know what? I'll grab a few things and we can eat at my place. If you want."

Super romantic. TV dinners for two? It's every girl's dream date!

Woah. Buddy. I take an actual step backward in reaction to my thoughts. *You're not involved with her, remember? So you don't care.*

"Oh! Well in that case, why don't you let me cook?" She tucks an escaped curl into her hat. "Come over when you're off work."

We're all standing in my construction zone of a bedroom in the same positions we held when this conversation started. Have I mentioned the super awkward tension? It's so thick I want to swipe my putty knife through it.

"Cool." She backs into the hallway.

John moves across my room. "Awesome." We exchange friendly but stilted good-byes and they leave together.

"Cool..." I speak to an empty room. Why do I feel like I've royally bungled a chance of a lifetime?

14

CORDELIA

LEA MICHELLE—IT'S THE MOST WONDERFUL TIME OF
THE YEAR

*H*e *didn't mean it. He didn't mean it. He didn't mean
it,* I chant down the stairs. Besides, there will be
more opportunities to see him. It's not like that was my one
chance of a lifetime to invite Gilbert to dinner.

As John and I step outside we both suck an instinctual
breath of self-preservation when the blood-thirsty Nebraska
wind bites our exposed skin. This deep cold shocks my
system—even when I think I'm prepared for it. This is frost-
bite-in-fifteen-minutes and farmers-losing-the-tips-of-their-
fingers kind of weather. This is can't-build-a-snowman-
because-the-snow-is-too-cold kind of weather. This is me
asking, "Why do I live where the air hurts my face?" kind of
weather. We slide past Gilbert's truck and John sprints to
his little blue car. I nod my head to acknowledge his wave as
he drives away.

The sun has about an hour of juice left. It heats nothing
but tortures us with a squinty, blinding reign of terror

against the white ground. I take slow breaths through my nose to heat the air before it burns my lungs. One of those thermal monkey cap ski masks would be nice about now. A balaclava. I could make baklava and eat it in my balaclava. And then of course I wonder if Gilbert could play a balalaika guitar thingy in the corner of the kitchen while this happens. I snort as the silly image pops into my mind as I scurry home.

The distance to the cottage has doubled since my last trip, and I barely make it to shelter before I die from the elements. I slam the door and lean my forehead against the cold kitchen wall. I've invited John to dinner, and I'm not sure how I feel about this.

Here's the thing about me, when I decide to do something, I do it. And when I discover it's not the best idea—perhaps not even a remotely good idea—I clean up my mess and get out.

I wanted to be in Australia, and somehow I landed in Svalbard, Norway. Of all the places I'd love to tour, it ain't Svalbard!

My cheeks bulge with the breath I hold, and I turn my back to the wall and slide to the floor. *Think, CJ!*

This is fine. I can work with this. John Brader is clever, talented. Fairly good-looking. He's got this blond hair that curls along the top and is trimmed short on the sides. We played a few games together yesterday—How was yesterday a week ago?—and got along well. He beat me once at Jenga.

The floor is cold beneath my leggings. I kick off my boots and haul myself to my feet. Sue me, I'm giving Svalbard a chance. I hear there are poisonous snakes in Australia. Spiders. Sharks. What kind of crazy person wants to swim in shark-infested waters? Deadly jellyfish? Not me!

I push away from the wall and march to the refrigerator. I'm not desperately looking for a boyfriend, ok? Especially not a rebound. But John requested *permission* from Gilbert to ask me out. We'll not think too deeply on why he felt the need to do that and if it speaks to a lack of confidence or some inappropriate bro-code of prior claim, but their conversation hung like a neon orange pinata that had been hit *just enough* to break open the sides and needed one more swing before all the candy fell out and *nobody reached for the bat.*

When nobody moves you can count on me to take one for the team. Every time. It is my innate sense of duty to step up to the plate when others don't.

I put it out there. I filled the silence. I broke the pinata, and we can move on.

There. I've come to terms with it. I'm not worried at all about this evening because I *like* to hang out with people, I *like* to go on dates, and I *like* food. *John is people, dates, and food.* I even and especially like first dates because Svalbard might be a fun new experience!

My internal debate coach does a roundoff triple back-handspring. I smile at her appreciatively. She has skills.

Why am I staring into the refrigerator? I'm not even hungry. I slam the door and turn a circle, unsure what I'm supposed to be doing.

Before I stumbled upon the world's most awkward conversation, the time tripped along merrily while I did ALL THE THINGS.

In town earlier I checked on Diana's crew. She says they're fine now, but tired. So I stealthily delivered a few grocery bags of new crayons and hot wheels, ginger tea, fuzzy socks, and a dozen other fun things I tossed in while shopping. I dropped a "You've been elfed" note in one of the bags. She'll know it was me because we used to "elf" people all winter long when we were kids.

Hmm. Gilbert would love that game.

Once home, I shuffled half the boxes from the kitchen to my room. Set up my kitchen, camera and accessories. Baked, staged, and photographed eight pies. I now have 1,083 shots to sift through. After I delete, adjust and edit, I'll have the handful I need for the final spread of the cookbook and five hundred to upload to the stock photo websites where I have accounts.

My publisher wouldn't love to find their copyrighted photos in a stock photo collection. But a butcher block countertop with flour dusted across the surface? The star of David drawn into that flour? "Happy Holidays" spelled out with chocolate chips? Those are all mine.

My master plan for tonight is to pull out easy-peasy deli sandwiches for dinner with John and serve him the photographed pies as our main course. In the meantime, I could be unpacking, setting up house, or washing dishes.

Nope. I am a potato.

I plop my rear into a chair at the cluttered table with my head cradled on one arm while I scroll Instagram.

Two hours later my phone buzzes.

Bing!

John: Have you seen the weather?

Cordelia: I see snow?

John: I feel like such an adult to bring this up. But I don't think it's smart for me to leave town. They're predicting high winds and blizzard conditions starting anytime and up to three feet by morning.

Cordelia: I've been in a pie factory all afternoon and I haven't crawled to the surface. I'm looking it up now.

Cordelia: Yea, it doesn't look good, mate. Guess I'll stay in Australia.

John: ?

Cordelia: Nevermind. Take a snow check?

John: Haha. Yea.

Cordelia: Eggnog cream pie, though. New favorite.

John: Save me a piece! You'll be okay? They might not get the roads cleared right away.

Cordelia: I stocked the bunker. No worries. Thanks.

John: Gotta finish closing. Talk later?

I spend the next five minutes searching for the perfect GIF of a girl secretly eating all the pie, but I never find it. Ah, well.

I do a quick YouTube search for "Australian dancing music." Aboriginal tribal videos with chanting, didgeridoos, and clapping spears are a sure mood enhancer.

My back pops when I curl my shoulders around. I slide from my chair and mimic the motions of those on the screen. *Stomp. Clap-clap. Stomp. Stomp. Clap-clap. Clap-clap.* I squat and shake my invisible spear in celebration. Would it have been fun to hang out with a new friend? Perhaps. But sleep is a delightful alternative after the adventures of last night.

I raise my spear and mentally chant.

What do we want? *Sleep!*

When do we want it? *Now!*

A slow grin spreads across my face as I boogie around my kitchen in wool socks. All flights to Svalbard have been rerouted.

Hold it. Wait right there.

Australia has never looked so good.

New plan.

The Aboriginal music grows obnoxious and I shut it off. I plant my feet with hands on hips while I stare through the window to think.

Gilbert doesn't want to date. *That's fine.* But I'm here and he's here and there is no reason that two people can't hang out and be friends. I like people. I like food.

I'm just a girl, standing in front of a phone, asking her landlord to come to dinner.

> Cordelia: I have a plethora of fresh baked desserts. Hungry? You should eat something.

> Gilbert: Who is this? I don't have this number saved.

> Cordelia: Oh, it's me.

> Gilbert: Grandma? When did you get a cell phone?

> Cordelia: Yep, I'm finally up with the times.

> Cordelia: *GIF of a cliche grandma looking through a magnifying glass*

> Gilbert: Cordelia Thompson, it's not nice to make fun of the elderly.

> Cordelia: Ha! You DID know it was me.

CHAPTER 14

Warmth steams through my core at his use of my full name, and I put it in my back pocket for later.

Gilbert: I'm saving your number.

Cordelia: Aunt Jewels gave me yours at the party.

Gilbert: Good ol' Aunt Jewels

Cordelia: And it was on the paperwork that Nickie had me sign.

Cordelia: You haven't seen this supposed paperwork have you? Brain exploding!! Is Nickie secretly running an evil genius renter's scheme under the table?

Cordelia: Does she sign all the checks over to herself and keep 80% as an executor's fee? How much control does she have??? How many other landlords is she scamming? Is she a slumlord for landlords??? Will I be found missing days from now and she'll have another double payment in her pocket from a new unsuspecting bloke from out of town???

Gilbert: Wow

Cordelia: Joke's on her anyway. I'm not so easy to take down.

Gilbert: She doesn't know about your extensive collection of black belts.

Cordelia: Them's facts.

Cordelia: How about it? You eat yet?

Gilbert: What happened to John? Didn't you have plans?

Cordelia: He's in Svalbard!

Gilbert: ?

Cordelia: Something about a blizzard? IDK.
Tsunami? Hurricane? High winds and a
bunch of white stuff?

Gilbert: Frozen precipitation?

Cordelia: *GIF of Bambi leaping and
disappearing into a pile of snow*

Gilbert: It would be remiss to let you eat a
plethora alone.

Cordelia: Nom nom nom

Gilbert: Thanks for the electric kettle.

Cordelia: YOU OPENED YOUR PRESENT!
ISN'T SHE PRETTY??? DID YOU USE IT
YET???

Gilbert: lol, I did. It made the water
super hot.

Cordelia: Literally her one job.

Gilbert: I burned the roof of my mouth.

Cordelia: I'm fixing you a plate. Get over
here.

Gilbert: Yes, ma'am

Cordelia: And bring your cello. I have
questions.

Gilbert: Cello questions?

Cordelia: Yessss

He doesn't reply and panic jumps on my back because I've been 100% *me* with Gilbert starting... when? When he tricked me into a driving lesson last night. Well, shucks. My rebrand isn't going so well.

But it doesn't matter. This *literal* Gilbert isn't looking for anyone to start a family with because he's building a house blah, blah, blah, and "too much needs done to play with girls."

No problem. *Figurative* Gilbert is still out there. I'll wait.

While I'm waiting for both aforementioned Gilberts to walk through my door, the hamsters spin their wheels. *I never called Mom today. Should I change into something nicer? It's weird not to have heard from Shaun at least once since the breakup. Does he even know that I've skipped town? Should I tell him? Why? Kinda thought I'd miss him more. This place would be cooler with a dishwasher. I guess most people living alone don't do as much cooking as I do. Lauren's going to love the little cross-stitch kit I bought her. I bet she's halfway done by now. I hope my roommates were able to find someone else to take my room. Can I say no if John asks me out again? Do I want to say no? Or am I wanting to say yes to someone else? Crap, I think I asked him out.*

I bounce over most of my scattered thoughts until I hit one that deserves an answer because she's so accusatory.

Stop obsessing over boys. Simmer down. It's not a crime to keep my eyes open for a potential husband.

Quit acting so desperate. I'm not! Making new friends is a good thing.

He doesn't want to be your boyfriend. Even better. I'll be normal and MAKE A NEW FRIEND.

What does that even mean? You've never been normal a day in your life. I don't have to explain myself to you.

Perhaps you have too many friends and nobody is serious about you because you're not serious? I'm not going to answer that.

Why don't you have more female friends? Ugh. Because most of my friends are married and have babies and I love that for them, but I'm not in that place.

Aren't you content in this season? Yes? Maybe? I don't know. Psh, that's not even a fair question. Ask any woman at any season if she's content in that season.

But ARE you? Sure. But I'd like to have... more.

More? Yes, more. Now move along.

My phone chimes a moment before a knock sounds a few feet from where I sit at the table.

> Gilbert: *GIF of Will Smith from 'Fresh
> Prince' knocking on the front door.*

I fling it open and a blast of winter flies inside.

He smiles. "Cordelia."

I smile. "Gilbert."

The hamsters go silent.

GILBERT

FRANK SINATRA—I GET A KICK OUT OF YOU

"May I come in?"

Cordelia blinks as if I've intruded on a private conversation.

"Please." She waves me forward.

The mess of hair piled on her head bounces when she steps to the side and I smile at her range of colors. Fuzzy red socks, sunshine-yellow leggings, green hoodie, and her vibrant hair outshines the rest.

The door shuts behind me, but my feet won't move. This woman is a magician of the best kind. My tired old kitchen has been transformed into a bakery. It's strange because some of the surfaces are magazine-level perfect and others speak of the industry behind the production.

The round table that used to be in the center of the room has been shoved aside, blocking the hall. This leaves room for two tripods with light umbrellas and a third tripod with a camera. One half of the table displays a placemat with a cluster of candles and a serving tray with slices of pie.

The rest of the table is strewn with papers, a laptop, a gray water bottle, and an open bag of jalapeño Cheetos.

Three pies inhabit the corner of the countertop with a dusting of powdery white stuff underneath and a wreath of holly leaves and sugared berries propped behind them. In stark contrast, the sink overflows with dirty bowls and dishes. By all appearances, the stacking method was designed by engineers with many letters behind their names and the addition of a single butterknife would send the modern art crashing to the floor.

"Wow," I say in a harmony of wonder and astonishment. "Wow."

She moves to stand beside me and hums a "what's all this?" sound as if she's here on official business. "There appears to have been a struggle." A pencil materializes in her hand and she taps it against her palm.

We stand in silence until she shoves the pencil into her wild bun and slaps her thighs. "Yep. All in a day's work." She pulls out the chair nearest the tray on the table and gestures to the tray of pie. "Hungry?"

Is there a man in his right mind who would say no?

We talk, and I eat as she disassembles her camera equipment. I help her move the table so she can store the tripods and camera bags in the hall closet. Cordelia has me talking about music, my instruments, and song preferences.

She never reminds me to call her CJ and this feels like a gift. I don't want to admit this, but that relaxed and peaceful feeling I had this morning returns. Interesting.

She moves throughout our long conversation. It doesn't appear to be anxious movement—she simply doesn't stop. By the time I've finished eating, the table's been cleared and wiped, leftover food covered, and she's halfway through hand washing the dishes.

"Can I help with that?" I set my plate on the counter.

"You're going to play. Is that weird to ask?" She smiles over her shoulder and a plate slips from her grasp, causing soap suds to speckle her face. "I only heard the one song at the party."

"I love to play." I dip my hands in her dish water, shoulder brushing hers, then dry them with the apron around her waist that she holds out for me. I brush my forearm down her cheek and catch the bubbles on my sleeve.

"What was that? Don't tell me I've had a streak of chocolate on my face this whole time."

"That or peanut butter."

Her eyes grow wide. "What?" In a rush, she scrubs the side of her face with the hem of her apron.

Laughing, I try to pull her hands away from her face. "I'm kidding! It was a bit of soap suds." Her hands disentangle from mine and then she whacks me on the shoulder.

"I don't even like peanut butter." She rubs her shoulder against her cheek. "Quit pestering and play some music, mister."

She chatters while I set up. I answer more questions than that time I brought the cello to the local second grade school party. But it's no hardship to speak about something I love as much as my music. My sliced arm is tight beneath the bandage but not painful, and I warm up my fingers with a simple scale. Cordelia stops talking mid-sentence, mouth agape.

Her gaze follows my fingers. "Lands to the living," she whispers. "That's incredible. Can you do it faster?"

I oblige, and she grins as if she's never witnessed anything more impressive in her life. Hanging out with Cordelia might be sinful for my ego. I point the bow at her.

"Stop grinning like that. I haven't done anything cool. It's a scale. It's one of the first things a musician learns." Her awed expression has me laughing to cover my flush at her delight.

"It looks cool." She reclines against the sink and crosses soapy arms around the middle of her green hoodie. "Do it again."

"You're not serious. Five-year-olds can do that."

"Do it." She points with her chin and her eyebrows jump. "Again." No messing around.

I've been playing the cello since middle school and leaned into it hardcore through high school. Maybe it started as a nerdy hobby, but when it turned into a job along with construction, I didn't care if it was odd.

I'm used to strangers being impressed. Although when they hear I also play the piano, guitar, and drums their praise can get annoying. But Cordelia's excited about a practice scale? I shake my head, a side grin pulling at my cheek. This will be fun. There's none of the adrenaline like when I'm on stage in front of ticket holders. I don't want to play Bach or a fancy concerto—and I've been playing Christmas music for weeks.

"No." I smirk at her defiant pout. Before she can interject—and it's obvious she wants to—I offer a broad smile. "Wait for it." I'll do her one better.

The sea shanty "The Wellerman" is one of the show-off pieces John and I perform. It's better with piano and box drum accompaniment, but the cello carries the meat of the song. I tap my heels in an alternating rhythm. *One-two. One-two. One-two. One-two.* Whatever she had on the tip of her tongue disappears when I jump into the opening, fingers working the strings by muscle memory.

She cocks her head. "I know this... where do I know

this?" Her foot taps as she watches my fingers dance along the strings. She starts to hum with the melody when I reach the chorus. "Dee, daa, de-da-da-da, to bring the sugar and tea and rum. Something, something da, da, da, as we go out to sea."

My laugh escapes when she butchers the words, and she bites her tongue between her teeth and crinkles her nose. Her face smooths and her pink lips relax into a natural smile. She's watching my fingers, and I'm glad I have this song settled deep in my memory because my concentration wavers. Her enraptured face pries open a sliver of pride in my work. When I finish an intricate phrase, she releases a breath.

"You're not even looking!" She steps closer and I stop playing, immediately distracted. And I don't want to bump her with an elbow. "How do you play it so quickly without even looking?"

"The strings don't move, Champ." I tap her on the head with the bow. "After all these years I think I know where they are."

She purses her lips in a don't-feed-me-a-line glare. "Do that part again."

I do, and she leans even closer. I'm an endangered species at the zoo that she's researching for science. She hasn't procured a magnifying glass, reference books, or a sketch pad yet, but I wouldn't be surprised to see them. I play through another verse and slip into an interlude of my own arrangement. If John was here, he'd take over the melody on the piano.

Halfway through the song, she steps away and I stretch into the music, letting myself sway from side to side and fill the space. Her eyes close with a smile and then she's dancing in the cramped corner of the kitchen.

It's the untrained, silly and free dance of someone who's simply moving. Enchanting. I need a jar to capture this spirit that she's released in this room and carry it home with me.

The song ends with a flourish, and I point the bow to the ceiling. She sighs, stepping to the sink. "I'm going to finish the dishes. Play another."

"Yes, ma'am."

The evening rushes by with more music and more food. Even though she put a proverbial spotlight on me, it's not too bright, and I enjoy sharing my music with her. That's what it feels like anyway. It doesn't sit awkwardly like an interview or a performance or "Hey, listen to me show off."

We enjoy the music together. We enjoy the food together.

I've put away the cello and now pick at a bag of chips because she won't let me help her clean. Anytime I rise to help with something she turns bossy with one word commands. "No," or "Sit." She points, like she's commanding a dog. Of course I obey. Thankfully I tucked my deck of cards in my coat and I busy myself with a game of Solitaire while we talk. Watching her flutter around the kitchen is entertaining.

She washes every dish and wipes the table and counter-tops. As if that weren't enough, she drops to her knees and washes the cabinet doors. After the sink is polished and dried she drops the rag on the floor and swishes it around with her foot. She unravels her bun—and gasps in surprise when, not one but three, pencils clatter to the floor—before she finally sinks into a chair next to me with her curls a delightful mane around her face. "What's your dream for the band?"

"What do you mean?"

"Well, you're over here building houses or something. Are you going to do that or play?"

That's the age-old question isn't it? I shrug. "I guess if we're dreaming I'd switch. Play full-time, build things for myself. But the music isn't as reliable. Everybody always needs something fixed."

"I make a living taking pictures of dessert. You just need a better manager."

I point my sock-covered toe and drag one of the pencils from the floor over to us. I pick it up and pass it to her.

She fiddles with the yellow pencil and smiles. "How do you know exactly where to slide your fingers on the strings?"

"We start with stickers, and after a while you just *know*. It's like whistling."

Her face falls. "I can't whistle."

"What? You poor thing. Show me." It turns out the girl *can* whistle, but can't control what sound comes out. An airy wind-through-a-drafty-window is the best she can do.

She surrenders with a shrug after a couple demonstrations. "My dad can do the high-pitched dog whistle thing. Doesn't even use his fingers."

I curl my tongue and show off my own "high-pitched dog whistle thing."

"Ack!" She covers her ears.

"Not everyone has the gene." I chuckle at her repeated failed attempts. "By spring you'll be driving a manual like a pro. That's enough to get in with the cool kids."

"Ha!" She slaps a hand through my piles of cards. "How many slices did you eat, Gilly-boy? Those pies didn't make themselves. I'm already a cool kid."

I tip my chair on two legs and thread my fingers behind

my head. "Hmm. I don't know... It's an elite group. We don't accept just anyone."

She leaps from her chair and presses her palm against my chest. My arms spread wide the moment the chair falls backward, then I grab her hand with my good arm. Her smug expression transforms to shock mid-fall and a shriek explodes into my ear as we crash.

Her weight sprawls across me for the barest moment before she tries to scramble away. But I'm not through yet. I pin her against my side and find her ribs. I know I've met my mark when she squeals.

"I'm sorry!" She gasps through her laughter.

"Did that go the way you thought it would go?" I speak through the red curls over my mouth.

"I'm sorry–Ow! Ow, ow, ow!"

I release her and she rolls away. She groans as she rises to her knees with a hand on her rear.

"What happened? Did I hurt you?"

Wavy locks of hair hide most of her face, but she's pinching her lips in an effort not to smile. "My butt." A giggle turns into a snort when she covers her face with both hands. "I'd forgotten I'd put—it was—there's a fork in my—" She can't even speak through the laughter, but reaches behind and pulls a metal fork from her pocket.

16

GILBERT

SATURDAY, DECEMBER 16

THE CARS—JUST WHAT I NEEDED

Last night was... huh. How do I classify last night?

I'm buried in a sleeping bag—no way I'm pulling out proper bedding until I'm done with the drywall mess—on my new-to-me mattress. I watch the glowing coals send a small plume of smoke up the open brick fireplace. The wind is a ravenous beast and there is not a glimmer of light from stars or sunrise through the window.

Last night was simply good. It was relaxed, comfortable... charged. I'm sure it was only the exciting newness that comes when you meet someone you click with. Born and raised in Hadley Springs, there haven't been many of those instances. Most people I come into contact with have known me since forever.

I roll on my back and tuck my hands behind my head. A goofy smile lingers, and I'm grateful there's nothing to capture how ridiculous I must look. Aunt Jewels would wiggle her eyebrows and crow, "I told you so!"

But... that's not what this is.

I'm allowed to make a friend. I can be platonic friends with a girl. Yeah, Cordelia is attractive, but there are plenty of attractive girls in town. She makes me laugh a lot, but so do *Lord of the Rings* memes on Reddit.

My five-thirty alarm buzzes from my cell across the room. Time for another exciting day.

Nothing happens when I flip the switch on the utility lamp. I turn on my phone's flashlight and the low battery alert flashes even though I'd plugged it in before bed. That means this is not a light issue, but an entire house electricity issue. If my house is out of power, the cottage is out of power. And if the cottage is out of power, Cordelia doesn't have any heat.

I throw scrap two-by-fours into the fireplace and work the dying coals into flames. By the light of the fireplace, I dress for a day of construction and snow shoveling.

Bing!

> Cordelia: Hey, hoser. You awake?

> Gilbert: Sup?

> Cordelia: I saw a light from your window.

> Gilbert: Let's pretend you're not standing at your kitchen sink staring at my window.

> Cordelia: If that makes you feel better.

> Cordelia: Gilbert Houston, we have a problem.

> Gilbert: It's Henry.

Cordelia: Mr. G. Henry Landlord, sir. I require your assistance. I think I broke something? IDK I woke up with a cold nose, your baby heater box won't turn on, and my night light in the bathroom went out and I'm scared to pee in the pitch black because there might be a badger hiding in the toilet.

Gilbert: Has that happened?!!

Cordelia: That's a very personal question, Mr. Landlord.

Gilbert: Have you looked into trauma therapy?

Cordelia: I have a candle, the badger situation has been averted.

Cordelia: Is there a breaker somewhere I should be flipping?

Gilbert: Remember those high winds? Frozen precipitation?

Cordelia: *GIF of Elsa letting down her hair*

Gilbert: A breaker won't help us. Power's down over here which means it's a frozen winter everywhere.

Cordelia: There's ice on the inside of the window. This is bad, yes?

Gilbert: The one you've been staring through waiting to see a light from my room?

Cordelia: No comment.

Gilbert: Start a drip in both sinks so our pipes don't freeze. Then come over here.

Cordelia: We can freeze together!

Gilbert: Or I can start my generator for lights, throw more wood on the fire and you can help hang drywall until they get the power back.

Cordelia: Start your kettle. I'll bring food.

Gilbert: Need help carrying anything?

Cordelia: You have coffee there?

Gilbert: Decaf instant powder

Cordelia: I think I just threw up in my mouth.

Gilbert: So… no? Is this a BYOC party?

Cordelia: You're so lucky I'm your neighbor.

Cordelia: French press. Check. Meat and cheese. Check. Crackers. Check.

Cordelia: What are you contributing to this party again?

Gilbert: I have the generator. Shelter. Power. There's water here.

Gilbert: And I have my own kettle!

Cordelia: I'm bringing my laptop bc I need to work. You'll have to drywall by your lonesome.

Cordelia: I opened the door and changed my mind. It's bad out there. Lost-in-the-prairie, find-my-corpse-in-a-haystack-next-summer bad.

Cordelia: I need a rope. Isn't that what we're supposed to do? Tie one end to a post and grope my way to the barn?

Cordelia: Sorry I said grope. That's gross. Nobody should use that word.

Cordelia: I could bring a candle with me, but the wind is evil.

Cordelia: Where's a metal pioneer lantern when you need one?

Cordelia: Hey. Watcha doin...?

Cordelia: Red rover, red rover. Send Gilbert right over!

CORDELIA

There's a scraping in the wild outdoors, but I can't see through the frosted window. I'm bundled tight—wool socks, leggings layered under jeans, shirt, hoodie, coat, gloves, hat, scarf, boots—and have managed to fit all the food stuffs in a canvas bag, and I stashed my laptop and notebook in my massive purse. *Phew.*

The knock at the door is muffled. I swing it wide to reveal Gilbert the Snow King dressed in brown coveralls with the collar raised, because he's the coolest kid in school. His fur-lined trapper hat snaps beneath his chin, and a thick layer of scruff protects his face.

The sight of him brings a smile to mine. "I'm saved!"

"Ready?" He steps inside along with swirls of snow and relieves me of both my bags. "You're about as cute as a bowl of plum pudding."

That wipes the smile from my face and I narrow my eyes.

He laughs. "What? I like plum pudding."

CHAPTER 17

Sure he does. Cute enough to look at. But not cute enough to date, marry, or have a family with. Sounds about right.

Doesn't matter. We can be friends, and I'll set up an online dating profile as soon as the internet returns. Plum pudding, bah! I need to find someone who thinks I'm alluring, charming, so gorgeous they wouldn't dare compare me to food. I've always wanted to check out the online dating scene. Why not have AI pair me with the perfect match? What could possibly go wrong?

"Red Leader Two, ready to launch?" He crouches enough to level his eyes with mine. "You okay?"

I muster a smile. "Let's go."

The thirty feet across the yard tries to kill me. I don't *think* it's still snowing, but the absurd wind produces snow clouds all over. And there's zero light. I could be following Gilbert into the great unknown. I'll be dead in ten minutes. Dead. Why do people live here on purpose?

I flounder in a thigh-high drift. The second time I fall, I screech in frustration. How is this happening? Gilbert's laugh fades in the distance.

"Gilbert!" The snow is loose enough that I've sunk almost to the ground, and I flop like a fish on the beach. "Gilbert?" Great. He's abandoned me to the elements.

This is it for me.

So long, world.

My numb lips struggle to form words. Still, I shout my complaints into the dark morning. "Leave me! Save yourself!" I manage to stand. "Have fun finding a new renter when word gets out that you've murdered me!"

My puffy coat restricts my ability to move my arms. "Third-degree murder is still a crime!" I'm completely disoriented. How long have I been out here? Three minutes? An hour? Five days?

It's far below zero and with the windchill I'm colder than I've ever been. I'm turning a slow circle with my hands clutching my hat against my ears when I'm swept off my feet by a lumbering bear that's materialized from a snow-cloud. "Oof!"

Gilbert flings me over his shoulder fireman style. "Third-degree murder?" He smacks my bottom through my coat, and I gasp. The nerve!

I yell to be heard over the wind. "What was I supposed to think?" I push my hands on his back and raise my head, but I don't struggle to get down. I'm not stupid. This free ride is uncomfortable but three levels up from walking through a blizzard. "You led me into the mist and abandoned me. That's bad—as bad as Gollum! Shelob could be right around the corner for all I could tell." Then I'm airborne.

I land in a snow drift. I am a starfish pressed into a plaster mold. "Gilbert Henry Conner!" I try to be stern, but my reproach ends with a laugh. I try again. "Gil—" Nope. I can't even get through his whole name without laughing. "I packed you—" I suck in a careful breath to still my laughter. "I HAVE COFFEE!"

His face appears over mine, grinning. "I already brought the coffee inside, sucker. Come in when you're ready to be civilized."

Before he moves, I fling a handful of snow into his face. A lot of difference it makes combined with the wind's efforts. But it gets my point across. Nobody backs Cordelia into a snowdrift and gets away with it. He smirks one last time and stomps up the stairs.

CORDELIA

SUNDAY, DECEMBER 17

KELLY CLARKSON—UNDERNEATH THE TREE

B*ing!*

> Cordelia: *GIF of the little boy from 'Up' waving "Hi!"*

Diana: *GIF of soldier in full gear lowering binoculars.*

> Cordelia: *GIF of Pooh Bear happy-dancing with a napkin around his neck, "What time is lunch?"*

Diana: You're braving the roads?

> Cordelia: *GIF of Legolas popping his head from a snow pile.*

Diana: lol, okay! Enough. You're such a child. I don't have time for this.

> Cordelia: *GIF of Dwight Schrute saying, "That's true."*

Diana: If I'm deciphering this correctly,
you're coming for lunch?

Cordelia: *GIF of Donald Trump speaking
into a microphone: "CORRECT"*

Diana: I'm turning off my phone in 10
seconds. I need to get my crew out the
door for church. And Mom says to please
return her calls.

Cordelia: Won't make it in time for church
today. The snow plow made a pass on the
gravel road and built a wall of ice blocking
our driveway. Mr. Landlord is shoveling.

Diana: You don't feel compelled to
help him?

Cordelia: Have you SEEN the muscles on
this machine? He could lift two of me on
one shovel. Me helping would be like Lisa
helping you cook.

Diana: Better view from the window?

Cordelia: That's not what I said.

Diana: So how's the view from the
window?

Cordelia: Ope, sorry. GTG. Water's boiling.
Toast is hot, um, the CAT NEEDS
FED! BYEE

❄

Bing!

Mark: FYI, my flight's on the 22nd at 7pm. Are you picking me up or do I order a ride?

Cordelia: No need for random car orders. We don't believe in them over here.

Mark: I've already looked it up. I can have one reserved.

Cordelia: What?! There's no way I'll let you pay that to get here. I'll pick you up.

Mark: You need to leave Hadley Springs by 5:30.

Cordelia: I can do math.

Mark: I don't want to be stranded at the airport again.

Cordelia: That was ONE TIME.

Mark: Put it in your calendar and I'll promise not to order a car.

Cordelia: *Screenshot of New Event in my calendar: "Pick up annoying cousin." December 22, 5:30 p.m.*

Mark: And set a reminder at least one hour before.

Cordelia: Done.

Mark: Good.

Mark: And be sure to get gas first.

Cordelia: Why? If I can make it to Omaha, then you can fill it up before we come home?

Mark: Sure, unless you don't make it, or you forget your wallet and then I'm stranded at the airport. Nvm, I'll order a car.

Cordelia: I'm kidding. We're good. I'll top it off just for you.

Mark: And I'm staying in Diana's guest bedroom. Please don't ask me again to sleep on the floor of your kitchen. I have standards.

Mark: I'm not sure how I ever survived growing up there. It's STILL below zero?

Cordelia: Nebraska…it's not for everyone.

Mark: How're you doing with work? On track?

Cordelia: Surprisingly, yes!

Cordelia: We were snowed in yesterday without any power and it's incredible how much I got done in one day of no internet.

Mark: WE were snowed in?

Cordelia: ME. I was snowed in.

Mark: You and Gilbert?

Cordelia: I WROTE LOTS OF WORDS WHILE I WAS SNOWED IN.

Mark: Why do I sense you're hiding something? Yelling your lies doesn't make them more believable.

Cordelia: I'm a devious trickster.

Cordelia: I have a sweet nugget of news actually. Call me later. I'm having lunch with Diana and the funny gremlins.

Mark: You're probably going to tell me now, aren't you?

Cordelia: I created my first ever online dating profile.

Mark: Here we go.

Cordelia: Unpalm your face. I look very professional in my picture. IDK. I'm very dateable in an "I'm an adult, but also the girl next door, but serious and focused, and definitely the kind of responsible human you want to start a family with" kind of way. I've already had a few, um, hits? From interested men.

Mark: That's oddly specific.

Mark: Be careful with that stuff.

Cordelia: I'm very careful all the time. Careful is my middle name. Cordelia Careful Thompson. People call me CC for short.

Mark: I'm not messing around. Don't jump into relationships with strangers.

Cordelia: Everyone is a stranger until you get to know them.

Mark: Yes. But you have a certain way about you that might give off the wrong impression, and I don't want people to take advantage of you.

Cordelia: K

Mark: I just want what's best for you.

Cordelia: Yep

Mark: Are you mad? Don't be mad.

Mark: Cordy. I know you're still reading these. Talk to me.

Cordelia: I'm not helpless.

Cordelia: Sure, I'm silly and WHATEVER but I'm not an idiot.

Mark: You're not an idiot.

Cordelia: Aren't you at church? We can talk later.

Mark: 2HR time difference, remember? And yes we WILL talk later. Aren't you at church?

Cordelia: House church. Can't get out of the driveway. Snow and stuff.

Mark: Be safe.

Cordelia: Stop saying that! What are you, my mom???????

Mark: Zipping…

Mark: JK. One more thing. For your house church: Proverbs 19:20: "Listen to advice and accept discipline, and at the end you will be counted among the wise."

Cordelia: You are LITERALLY the worst. Go bug someone else. BYE.

Mark: Don't tell any of the online people where you live.

Cordelia: BYEEE

Mark: Promise me.

Cordelia: Yes, okay, fine. No telling good-looking men that I meet online where I live because that would be moronic.

Cordelia: I'M NOT AN IDIOT.

Bing!

Gilbert: Morning, Champ. I know it's too late for church. Sorry I didn't get the drive unblocked earlier, but it's clear now.

Cordelia: Oh! Awesome. Thanks. I didn't realize you were out there, I would have joined you.

Gilbert: Should I pretend I didn't see you watching from the kitchen window?

Cordelia: Gah! They're on to me. Who keeps ratting me out???

Gilbert: *GIF of Michael Scott peeking through window blinds*

Cordelia: I'm having lunch with Diana and the gang, want to come?

Gilbert: *Typing bubbles appear and disappear*

Cordelia: There's plenty of food. And of course I'm bringing my leftovers from work.

Gilbert: You have the coolest job.

Cordelia: *GIF of the animated Alice in her blue dress and white apron dipping into a prim curtsy*

Gilbert: I usually have Sunday lunch with Aunt J

Gilbert: *Typing bubbles appear and disappear.*

Gilbert: Can't join you this week. Want to ride together? I can drop you off at least. No sense taking two cars into town.

Cordelia: We can have a driving lesson in the daylight when you're not bleeding everywhere??

Cordelia: Yaasss. Come out at 11:30.

Gilbert: Will do.

Cordelia: ALSO!! Oh my word. As weird as this shower is, I have one and you don't. What do you have to say for yourself? You have permission to use this one.

Gilbert: Can you smell me from there? Through the thermal shirt and coveralls?

Cordelia: Weirdo.

Gilbert: Appreciate the offer, but Aunt J has a fantastic bathroom. I'll make use of it.

Cordelia: Like, every day?

Gilbert: It's motivation to keep trucking. I finished installing the water heater last night. Bathroom tile begins tmw. Should have a working shower in 4 days.

Cordelia: My thumbs are tired. Can I come over? I'm all sad and lonely. Have the scouts returned? Is it safe to traverse from my camp to yours?

Gilbert: I'll make you hold drywall.

Cordelia: Still?

Gilbert: Drywall is like that and every hour I care less. Must. Get. It. Done.

Cordelia: Be right there.

Gilbert: BYOC

Cordelia: Understood.

Gilbert: It feels wrong not to be in church, but rolling in 45 minutes late? How do you feel about sharing communion with me?

Cordelia: I'll bring pie crust!

Gilbert: I have grape soda.

Cordelia: See you in a sec.

CORDELIA

WEDNESDAY, DECEMBER 20

THE FONTANE SISTERS—NUTTIN' FOR CHRISTMAS

"Eww!" I yell around a mouthful of popcorn.

My fuzzy blue-slippered feet are propped on the coffee table in Diana's living room and two-year-old Lisa snuggles in my lap. It's late, and I've been here for hours. Buddy the Elf stuffs his mouth with previously chewed gum from New York's streets.

Lisa claps her hands.

"No, baby. We say, 'Boo!' No eating gum off the street."

She giggles in response.

"Boys?" I spear the twins squished on either side of me with an inquisitive stare. "You're walking along the street and see free gum. What do you do?"

"Eat it!" Now they're just messing with Aunt Cordy. They can't stop laughing at my extreme faces of horror.

Lauren glares over her shoulder from the end of the wrap-around couch."Shh. You're ruining the show."

"Sorry." I nudge the twins. "You're getting us in trouble." We're very good and quiet for another twenty minutes until Diana walks in with a laundry basket on her hip and a phone to her ear.

"Everyone say hi to Grandma." She pauses the movie while the kids yell unintelligible greetings toward the phone. "Cordy says hi too. Yeah, she's good." Diana stares through me. "I'll tell her. Love you, Mom. Got to go." After shoving the phone in her back pocket she gestures to the kids. "Bedtime! We'll finish the rest tomorrow."

The boys start to fuss until I clamp my hands on their knees. One more squeak and they know I'll enact judgment. "Yes, Mom." I remind them. "Come on, the first one to bed gets a penny. Ready, go!"

They scramble across the living room, shoving and pushing each other. Lance falls on the speckled cream-colored carpet and latches onto Leo's foot, then they're both crawling into the hallway like baboons.

Now that the roads are mostly plowed and nobody's throwing up, I intend to be here most evenings. Working from home has its perks, but I was not born to spend endless hours by myself. I plan to be such a constant in these kids' lives that they'll wonder what I'm doing when I'm not here.

Diana scoops Lisa from my lap. "Five minutes, and then you're showing me the dates you've set up."

I squint and tilt my head like I don't understand her perfectly clear command. "Dates? We're all going to Aunt Jewels' tomorrow... She hosts on Thursdays, right? Hmm... and my project is due on the twenty-second. Those dates?"

Diana ogles as if I've forgotten to put on a shirt. "Your app thing." She waves at my waist. I assume she's motioning to where she thinks my phone is tucked in my pocket.

"The app thing?" I prop my chin on my fist because I am a philosopher working to decipher her odd request. "You'll need to be more specific."

She squeezes the white laundry basket against her hip until the plastic bends. "Putting yourself out there again? Finding boys to take you on dates like some kind of desperate woman?"

Okay. Tell me how you really feel, Diana. "I haven't been on any dates since Shaun." I screw up my face in confusion. It's dramatic, but I think she's still buying it.

Lisa burrows into Diana's neck and the basket of socks and rags dumps on the couch. Diana waves her free hand in a circle around her ear. The wheels are turning. She's almost got it. "You know. The—" She lets out an exasperated sigh. "I can't *think* anymore. My brain turns to mush when I need it to produce the proper name of anything."

"Mom brain." I hum sympathetically. "Sounds terrible. Maybe you should go to bed and forget about it for tonight."

"But you *know* what I'm talking about."

I shake my head, eyebrows raised. She'll never crack me. I offer her popcorn, but she scowls.

Her *mom brain* isn't inhibiting the *mom stare* I'm receiving at the moment. "Five minutes." She points. "Don't go anywhere."

Over her shoulder she shoots out one more command. "And no more bribes. You owe all of my kids a penny."

At the kitchen table I open my laptop and login to my profile on the Friendly Fish dating site. There are three new messages since this morning. One from a David K.

> David: Hi, CJ! Your job sounds incredibly fulfilling. I'm interested in getting to know you better. Check out my profile.

I click his name.

Well, well, well. David K. Dark, thick hair artfully swooped out of his handsome eyes. Strong nose and kind smile. Navy sweater with a white line around the V-neck, hands casually tucked in his jean pockets. His profile reads, "Doing > Dawdling. Motion > Meddling. Coffee > Tea. Sleep > Scrolling."

Well, nothing as fascinating as "goat wrangler from the alps" or "flight instructor from Hawaii," but since he started the conversation, I'll chat. I answer with a simple "Hi" and he pings back almost immediately. He's pleasant, if a bit stiff. Our conversation moves along because I ask him questions about his line of work. Most men love to talk about that. He's a home inspector in Omaha. Good money, flexible hours. Gets to carry a tablet around everywhere he goes.

> Cordelia: Wow. That must make you feel really important.

> David: Why's that?

> Cordelia: Oh, nvm. Just a joke on how those in management positions seem to always be walking around with tablets. Like the old clipboard cliche. Isn't that a thing anymore?

> David: Gotcha. Haha. Yea, I guess. That's me, Clipboard Guy.

A sigh leaks out before I stop it.

"Show me the goods." Diana slips into the chair next to me.

I have the impulse to close all my tabs and snap the laptop shut.

Here goes.

Using one finger, I nudge the corner of the laptop ever so slowly until it's facing her.

A high bun captures her dirty-blond hair and tendrils fall around her face. Even exhausted, she's stunning. Eyes track and her lips silently move as she skims the page. Every few seconds an eye-brow twitches. Once, she glances at me, and her expression says, "Really?"

I tap my fingers on the underside of the table and wait for her to finish snooping.

She closes the screen and rests her hands on it. She smiles softly.

My palms sweat. "What?"

"You need to delete this."

"What! Why? I worked really hard setting that up. I picked every word of my bio with care. Compelling but discreet. Cautious not to give away too much but still appearing welcoming and open." My speech bounces off her shields. "An online dating profile is essentially an ad to market yourself, and I'm... well, extremely clickable."

She shakes her head.

"What's wrong with it?"

"This girl sounds interesting, Cordy. But she isn't you." She reaches toward me, but I'm on my feet in a moment pacing the side of her dining room. I don't want to look at her pity.

CORDELIA

JUDY GARLAND—HAVE YOURSELF A MERRY LITTLE
CHRISTMAS

Nathan enters the side door, leather bag slung across his chest and black Oxfords wet with snow. "Hey, Babe. Is there food? Please, tell me there's food." He wipes his shoes on the entry rug. "I'm minutes from selling my birthright for a soup." Nathan looks up then lifts his chin to acknowledge me at the table. "Hey, Squirt."

"Hey, Spreadsheet." I was seventeen when Nathan and I first met. Although I don't have anything against my brother-in-law anymore, our first meeting involved a prolonged argument over who knew Diana best—super mature, I know—and neither of us have offered more than polite animosity since.

"That's a new one." He winks at Diana. "Tough day at the office?"

"Whenever I'm feeling down, I think how grateful I am that I'm not in *your* office." I quirk my lips to the side, unsure if that was too far even as he ignores me and approaches my sister.

He shrugs out of his coat and kisses Diana. It's not a polite peck on the cheek if you know what I mean. *Gag.*

"Meeting ran late." He trails a finger down the side of her neck, and I look away. That touch is more heated than their kiss. "But I'm taking a half-day tomorrow. Can you have them dressed for sledding by one-thirty?"

Her tired smile is all hearts and bubbles. "They'll love that."

"What did I interrupt?" He jerks his thumb toward my laptop.

"Nope. Nothing. Nada." I shake my head while grabbing my laptop, but Nathan is quick as a viper and he snatches it from my grasp. I screech and slap his arm. "So help me, Nathan. It doesn't concern you."

There's a blast of fire in my tone that leaves all fun and games behind. His concerned gaze snaps to mine, and he slowly sets it down. Hands in the air, eyebrows low, Nathan steps away from the table.

I suck in my lip and stalk into the living room to escape Nathan's wide-eyed stare. While I forcefully shake my hands to expel the overflow of anguish that hits me from nowhere, I pace twice in front of the large TV. I am not okay and I don't know why. I want to bite something and I'm so embarrassed for attacking Nathan.

Writing conferences, publishing contracts, photography awards—I've made a good living since college with words and art. Partly because my work is unique and bright and compelling, and partly because I'm a machine that never slows down. Throw a thousand darts and a few of them are bound to hit home.

The past decade I've attended friends' weddings all

over the country with various plus-ones at my side. Can you believe a sickening number of those couples have already divorced? For two years I was trapped in what turned out to be a dead-end relationship while working overtime to advance my career.

I want... I want *more*. But I don't know what. I'm reaching for something that eludes me. Letting Nathan see my weaknesses spilled out would only push me deeper into my dark corner. As long as I pretend to be this confident, adventurous girl who's unafraid of life then everything will be fine.

I *am* confident and adventurous. But lately I feel small. Insignificant.

A giant's foot looms above me. I'm running and running, but the foot comes ever closer to crushing me.

I drop to the carpet and gather Jack's toys into his basket. I line up the little pairs of shoes in front of the TV and make a pile of their picture books on the coffee table. My breath is running fast like I've been army crawling under the pews during church tag.

Nathan and Diana were the dream couple that met the first week of college and married a year later. They had Lauren before Diana's junior year—the year Nathan opened his insurance business in Hadley Springs and moved them away from where I'd just started at UNK. Diana managed to graduate by taking online classes.

Nathan stole my sister from me.

My big sister will never understand what it's like to be me. She can't relate to the decisions I've had to make. Nathan has been her rock for eleven years. For *eleven years* she's had him to talk to and make plans with. This entire decade she's been lucky enough to wake up next to a best friend and share her thoughts.

I want that level of trust with someone.

I've put the living room to rights, and the corner of the gray sectional is as far as I can get away. I toss the fleece blanket over my head and curl into myself. In my cave, I scrub my face in my hands and wish it all away. I made a fool of myself in front of Nathan. Where's the button to rewrite the past five minutes?

God, am I chasing a dream that isn't for me? Is it wrong to take an active step in planning my future?

The couch dips beside me.

I bury my fingers in my hair and pull to the point of pain, needing a physical distraction before I explode.

A throat clears—Nathan—and I peek from the blanket.

He's not looking at me, my closed laptop in his hands. "Diana suggested that I—well, that I—raise a white flag? I don't know. I'm... sorry. I thought our constant teasing was harmless. Only teasing. But if I've taken it too far, or offended you... I'm sorry." He holds up the computer. "I would never pry into your life. You don't have to explain anything, defend your decisions, or be afraid of me. I've only ever wanted good things for you. I think you're amazing, and I'd do just about anything for you. Diana, the kids, and you. You're in the top three, Cordy."

Diana hovers by the end of the couch with tears in her eyes. Cautious. I feel rotten that my sister is hesitant to approach me. "Will you trust him to read your profile? I think another pair of eyes would be helpful."

I flip open the screen and return it to him. I stare at the far wall. If he's surprised, he hides it well. He reads through my dating profile twice as fast as Diana did. They share a glance before he settles his contemplative gaze on me. I wave Diana over and she sits on my right.

She straightens the blanket around my knees.

I kick it off.

She picks it off the floor and folds it into quarters.

"You're both a bunch of clipboards." I slump farther into the corner. "Just get on with it. I promise I can take it." Big talk coming from a girl who fled a minute ago.

Nathan leans forward. "We—Diana and I—we don't think there's anything wrong with online dating. We have nothing against it. It's a great way to meet like-minded people who are outside of your regular locations. How else would you meet um—" He glances at the screen. "David the home inspector from Omaha, who might be your perfect match? But we worry you're conforming into someone that's not you. You haven't lied in your profile, but it paints a different picture than who we know you to be."

I'm boneless and melt off the couch onto the floor. "My profile is perfect." I speak to the underside of the coffee table. "See for yourself how many clicks I got over the weekend."

Nathan chuckles. "I see that. Very impressive. Did you notice all of these men are wearing suits or Old Navy sweaters? They don't—"

I pop from the floor, narrowly missing the table. "Look at yourself! You with your khakis and your collared button-ups. You're wearing a sweater vest! You're dressed for a family photo shoot with your Grandma every day."

"Cordelia!" Diana calms only when Nathan rests a hand on her arm. I'm a pouty child. I cross my arms and pinch the flesh around my rib. The sharp pain redirects enough energy that I can keep my mouth shut.

Nathan grins. "You're right, but you and I would never have made a good match. There's a reason Diana caught me. You're—"

"I'm not the kind of girl men want to have families with. I get it." There. I've said it out loud.

"What?" Nathan and Diana speak together.

Diana recovers first. "That's nonsense."

I retrieve my laptop and tuck it under my arm, ready to storm out of here and escape this suffocating house.

She rescues my computer from my crushing grip and tucks it into my purse. "Why would you say that?"

"Nevermind. It's nothing." I bolt for the door. I don't need to explain how Shaun's parting words brought to light what I've always known. I shove my feet into my snow boots.

"It's not nothing, if that's how you feel, we need to—"

I'm out the door and halfway to my car before Diana catches up. "Cordy, wait."

"What?" The cold bites my hands. I count the icicles along the edge of the roof.

"We love you." She hands me my coat and scarf.

There are twelve icicles, though the largest one has lost its tip. I yank my gloves from the coat pocket. "Yep."

"See you tomorrow?"

"Yep."

The drive home is a blur. Parked by the cottage, I sit in my car with no plans to gather my stuff and walk inside. At some point I put on my coat. Hands on the steering wheel, gaze unfocused, I let my thoughts run amok.

I'll schedule a meetup with David K. and get it out of my system. Nathan's absolutely right. Those men won't want me after we meet. I will have tried. Put forth the effort. Is this David the Gilbert to my Anne? I think not, but he's pleasant.

Maybe I'll turn a new leaf.

Maybe I like a man in a suit.

My cell buzzes with a new text message, and I ignore it. Tomorrow I'll roll out of bed at five and read through my final cookbook draft with a fine-tooth comb before I hand it over to my editor by noon. That'll be a wrap on *Christmas Comforts: Desserts*. By next October it'll grace shelves all over the country. This time I'll get my name in bold along the bottom. Maybe a picture of myself on the inside flap. This baby was mine from conception. I'm not just a staff photographer anymore.

It's been an all consuming project. I have been cooking for the Christmas season an entire year. *Christmas Comforts: Timeless Sides*, *Christmas Comforts: Breads*, *Christmas Comforts: Main Courses*.

Snowflakes gather on my windshield.

I should be elated. This time tomorrow I'll be done. Not only done, but a full day ahead of schedule. I rest my head against the steering wheel.

Go me.

GILBERT

A-HA—TAKE ON ME

My text to Cordelia remains unanswered and she's yet to exit her car. I've noticed the past week that she's in the habit of sitting there a few minutes after shutting off the engine. But this evening it's far too cold to stay out for long. I tap the screen again just to be sure.

> Gilbert: You alive?

I've been playing with dry-wall mud all day. I'm going with a knock-down texture in every room because I don't want to mess with the dust of sanding during a season when I can't open the windows. Steamy water runs over my hands while I scrub my tools in the stainless steel kitchen sink. Her car is in my line of sight from the kitchen window—I'm not a creep.

Hot water from the faucet is officially my new favorite thing. As soon as our HVAC guy, Royce, can spare a minute, he'll wire the furnace.

Cordelia hasn't moved from her car. I shut off the tap and fumble for the terrycloth towel draped over my counterless cabinets.

Because I'm not a stalker, I turn from the window and lean against the sink. Blinds might need to go up before I finish the walls if I can't keep my eyes off the cottage and the girl next door.

Around this point in every project I imagine that I'm almost done. The only thing left to do is texture walls, hang cabinets, install countertops, lay flooring downstairs, prime everything, paint everything, tile bathrooms and kitchen backsplash, install baseboards, trim windows and doors, install light fixtures, bring in appliances, hang the rest of the new doors...

Right, then. I'm not almost done.

At some point the dim outline of her Toyota and the dark cottage returned to my line of sight. She's been out there forty-five minutes. This isn't normal. Or healthy. Concern for her wellbeing overpowers me. I switch off the utility light in the kitchen, shove my arms into my coat, and walk out the door before I talk myself out of it.

She's slumped forward in her seat with her head against the steering wheel. Is she breathing? Adrenaline spikes my chest, and I rip open the door. Cordelia doesn't move.

"Hey." My breath fogs the night air. "You alright?"

I squat down to her level as she turns her face to me. Her lips are tinged blue. "Go away."

"Uhh, no. No, I will not."

"I'm fine."

I hook my hand under her arm and attempt to tug her from the car. "Don't tell me lies, ma'am. No sane person sits outside in this weather."

The mew of a lonely kitten leaks from her mouth, but

she doesn't pull away. "Not you too." Her legs are criss-crossed on the seat, snow boots abandoned on the floor-board. "I'm not crazy," she says while struggling to uncross her legs.

"Of course not. That's why you planned to sleep in your car and die of hypothermia."

"Lemme alone." Her words are weak-willed enough that I'm seriously worried. This isn't Cordelia. "I can take care of myself."

"Prove it." Anger nips at my words. How long would she have stayed out here? Despite her bold claims, she leans into my hand.

"My leg's asleep."

My patience gives out, and I scoop her from the car. Cordelia squeaks but doesn't fight when I cradle her against my chest.

"It'll be much too hard—" I knock the car door shut with my boot. "—to find a new renter when—what was it you threw at me? When word gets out that I've murdered you?" With her hands flung around my neck, I carry her to the front door. "Securing a tenant who bakes pies and cookies and is game for midnight runs to the hospital is a difficult feat." As is opening a door with a woman in my arms.

Her lack of snappy comebacks astounds me. "Cordelia." I wait for her to look at me. "Hey."

She burrows her head against my shoulder.

A package blocks the entry, and I kick it inside the dark room. Once I have her situated in a kitchen chair, I turn up the space heater and refill her electric kettle. Her head pillows in her arms on the table.

Is this where I leave? She's inside. She won't die. Obviously she's not feeling well, but she's an adult and can take care of herself. If she needed my help she'd ask for it. After all, she's not my responsibility. Not my family. We're hardly friends.

Except. Yes, we are. One swipe through our texts proves that much. Even if we've only been friends since two a.m. five days ago.

If I were in her place what would I need? My mind blanks. I've never stayed in my truck until my lips turned blue and my feet fell asleep. If I did, I'd be so embarrassed that I'd insist on being left alone.

Not gonna happen.

I rifle through her cupboards and drawers until I find a box of peppermint tea and prepare two cups. Two will make it less awkward. Two friends having tea. We don't have to talk. I'll just sit there until—until I decide she's okay. Makes perfect sense.

She doesn't move when I pull out a chair and sit beside her. Did she fall asleep? Is she hiding from me? Maybe I should just go. I wish I hadn't put her down. Then at least she'd be warmer. And I liked holding her. Next time I'll bring her inside and sit with her in my lap.

Next time?

Two friends having tea. Even if one of them is pretending to be asleep. This isn't strange at all. I dig my phone from my front pocket for backup.

> Gilbert: Hey

Nathan: Sup

> Gilbert: Nvm

Nathan: Aight

That was dumb. I don't need Nathan's advice about Cordelia. Although I'd like to know how worried I should be. Is this sleep-it-off level girl drama or something more serious?

My phone vibrates before I've put it away.

> Nathan: Diana wants to know if Cordy made it home.
>
> Nathan: I told her you aren't her sister's keeper, but can you check?

> > Gilbert: I'm with her. Sort of. She's being weird.
> >
> > Gilbert: Not weird but quiet.

> Nathan: That's weird for Cordy.
>
> Nathan: Diana says that's inappropriate and you shouldn't be alone together.

> > Gilbert: Tell Diana I'm a saint.

> Nathan: She says so is Augustine.

> > Gilbert: ?

> Nathan: IDK, I'm just the messenger.
>
> Nathan: Diana also says Cordy does the quiet thing sometimes. She'll be fine.

> > Gilbert: Ok

I'm less anxious but a blast of hot anger shoots through me instead. Diana knows this happens and hadn't bothered to check on her sister until I reached out to Nate? My text jogged Diana's memory that she has a family member in bad enough shape she may not have made it home? Did she have a *clue* that Cordelia would sit in the car to the point of hypothermia? It's still below zero out there.

I'm not about to leave Cordelia in this state. Someone

who'll stay in the cold until they can't move cannot be trusted to care for themselves. My brother Cameron used to have mood swings similar to this. Hm. Once he didn't shower or leave the house for over a week. Can't be having that.

"Okay, Champ." I clap my hands once, and she lifts her head with a scowl. "Pity party's over."

She huffs, the sides of her mouth turned down, but glances at her mug of tea. "I'm not having any kind of party."

"Sure you are. I don't know what about. But by all accounts you've spiraled into a weird slump, and I don't see you climbing out anytime soon. I'm here. Let's do this."

She unzips her coat. "Sounds like you have everything figured out, Coach."

Fine. I can be Coach. If I ignore the ugly tone of her voice. I clear my throat. "What set you off?" Maybe if I get her talking, it'll help. I wonder if sitting beside her is intimidating. The box on the floor has begun to absorb water from the snow I tracked in. I place it on the table. "Shall we see what's in here?"

"It's the showerhead." Not the least bit excited.

Wow, she's fallen hard. "Awesome. I'll install it for you tonight."

"Whatever."

I snap open the top of the box and mimic her with extra snark. "Whatever!" Whistling in amazement, I unpack everything. "Now would ya look at this? It comes with a detachable hose. You picked a good one. This brushed nickel will look really nice."

"Listen, Gilbert..."

I'm very interested in unloading the box. What have we

here? I've never seen a showerhead and must examine it from all angles.

"I don't know what you're doing here. You're very annoying. Asking what set me off?" Her whiny voice reminds me of Nate's oldest girl, Lauren. "Nothing set me off. I'm not some kind of machine. An uncontrollable device that malfunctions willy-nilly? That's insulting. I'm sad. Okay? I'm annoyed. I'm angry." Her whimper is both pathetic and laughable. "I'm in the depths of despair."

She's told me to scram, yet she's still talking. Maybe I should stay but be cool about it. More friend, less coach?

Got it.

The showerhead instructions are in four different languages. I slowly open the accordion of gibberish and avoid giving too much attention to her. Just a handyman neighbor friend drinking tea and installing stuff. Let's pretend that I'm the kind of man who normally reads instructions in detail. Hahaha. What a good actor I am.

"It's stupid, and I'm stupid and everyone is a moron." Cordelia shoves her mug and hisses when the hot tea splashes the back of her hand. With that hand to her mouth, she drags the cup back. "I think it would be better if you left because I'm bound to say something mean, and I don't want to hurt your feelings."

There we go. Well, then. If that's all she's worried about, we're getting somewhere. "I'm known around these parts for my hard shell." I knock a fist against my chest. "Shields of steel and such. Tough guy right here." Too much? Okay. I purse my lips in what I hope is a thoughtful expression and not my poor attempt to keep from laughing at her apparent distress. If I look at her I will cave. That would be very rude.

These instructions are simply fascinating. I squint at the miniscule print.

Cordelia smacks the paper out of my hands. "Oh, shut up. Now you're patronizing me."

I grab her hand before she tosses the instructions to the floor. "Listen, missy." I attempt to pry her fingers from the mini booklet. It occurs to me that I have limited experience comforting women in times of distress. If I'm reading the signs correctly—and with my track record of the evening I'm probably not—it's clear she wants to fight. If it were Cameron I'd knock him out of his chair, he'd punch me back, and then we'd move on. Probably shouldn't try that one.

I speak slowly. "My brother goes through these cycles where he's up and happy and ready to take on the world one week, then hates everything and everyone the next." She doesn't release the booklet, and I pull each finger off the pages one at a time. "I'm not bringing him up to compare or anything. All I meant is that whatever you've got to say it's not gonna freak me out. And putting it all out there—out loud—could help." I scan the counters. "Or you can write it. Surely you have paper? Cameron meets with a counselor, and I'm not—I don't mean anything by that, but I'm just saying. Sometimes people process life differently and can use some help and that's—that's fine."

Her fingers go limp in mine. Now I'm just holding her hand. When I eventually glance at her, she's pressing the rim of her mug against her lips with her other hand.

After three full seconds her ice sculpture melts, and she takes a sip, gaze drilling a hole through me, one hand in mine the whole time. "Do you mean me? Or... people... in general?"

I slowly straighten my spine and move slightly away.

Her mug slams on the table and more tea splashes across her hand. "You meant me! You think I... that I... what? That I'm crazy? I don't need a shrink." Her gaze darts around the room then lands on our touching palms. "Why are you holding my hand?"

"I'm not." I thread my fingers through hers. "This is holding your hand."

"You're acting weird."

"Yes, I'm very weird." Backpedal. Reverse. Start over. "Wanna play cards?" I fish into the inside pocket of my coat and grab the deck with my free hand.

She shakes her hand from mine while tossing me a confused glance. "You carry a deck of cards with you at all times?" Her voice pitches lower into a strange salesman accent. "Never fear! Weirdo Gilbert is here with his colorful pieces of printed paper. They will wipe all your troubles away. Come one and all and witness the amazing trouble-wiping cards of Master Gilbert."

I deal us nine cards each.

She fake gags. "Ugh, no. I don't wanna play your stupid game."

"Jackie Wins. It's not stupid. You're stupid, and I'm stupid, and everybody is a moron. Remember? Place three cards down in a line, three facing up on top of them, and keep three in your hand. For the first round, don't worry about which ones."

"The game is called Jackie Wins?"

"Yes, ma'am."

The cards I've dealt her seem to be invisible. Her fingers curl around her mug. "Explain."

"It will be easier if I wait until you're set up, but okay.

The first to play all their cards wins. We take turns discarding. Twos are wild. Fours are really good, keep those, and tens restart the pile. When you play your hand, you want to start with your lowest cards because we play up. If you can't play, you pick up the pile. When your hand is empty, you play from your cards on the table. Face up first, and then the hidden cards. It's an unlucky surprise if you have a three under there."

A glazed expression clouds her face.

"I thought it might be easier to talk while we're doing something with our hands. Go ahead and lay out the three—"

"*Explain* why it's called Jackie Wins. I have no idea what you just said."

I chuckle. "John's cousin, Jackie, always wins. Always. We started calling it Jackie Wins and so does everybody else. Nobody remembers the real name."

Cordelia places her hand over her cards and moves them to the edge of the table until they fall on the ground. "Oops." She doesn't even look where they fell.

Cool. If she wants to fight, I can fight. "You're being a jerk. You know that?" I flick a card into her face.

A blink. That's the most I get from her. She removes her hairband and shakes out her tangled mess of curls. "Yeah. Probably. Is it worse than cute and fun? Maybe it's best. I could try to be really good and make sure people like me, except then they still don't and they—they ask me to marry them and everything should be wonderful." She claps her hands together in front of my face with a forceful *smack*. "But it's not wonderful, Gilbert. It's not wonderful because Shaun doesn't want me. Why would he?"

Shaun, the ex-boyfriend? Ex-fiancé? I clear my throat to

make a show of having something to say, but she continues without my help.

"I'm obviously not what men want. Not for keeps anyway." She retrieves the single card from her lap and tries to throw it at me like a frisbee. "But I don't even care!" The card sails behind my chair. "I don't care about Shaun. And what kind of monster does that make me? Shouldn't I miss him?" Her voice quavers. "Shouldn't I miss his face? Or his kisses or something? We barely hung out once a week because the commute across town was a hassle. Oh my word! You'd think that would've been a sign. I've seen you every day this week. For clocked hours, it's as much as I'd seen Shaun in two months."

I raise my eyebrows, and she scowls as if this is my fault. Thankfully my shields are still in place.

"I dated the guy almost two years, and we—well, I guess I thought he loved me. Good joke, yeah? We said the words. But how could he?" She sweeps her arms wide, and her gestures speed along with her words. "It's clear I didn't love *him* because I don't miss him. I'm over here crying because I'm lonely and all broken-up, but good grief! Can you think for one ever-loving minute what might have happened if we'd gotten married? What a mess. What a stinking awful mess that would've been."

I'm very still. I hold the deck together mid-shuffle while she looks at me with tear-filled eyes. My thoughts careen back to the part where she said she's not what men want. Who are these men, anyway?

"How could Shaun love me when he didn't know me? I was really fun. So fun. I was happy all the time but it wasn't good enough. So you know what that makes me? A terrible person." The sides of her mouth quiver, and she continues to shake her head. "I'm a rotten, despicable person. Here you are trying to be nice. Why are you here? I'm the worst company. Then when you explain the rules to a card game, I'm so insanely annoyed." She forms bear claws and grips the side of her face. "So annoyed with you because I can't remember a freaking thing you said about the cards, and I don't want to play a stupid card game. Why am I so mad? I want to physically hurt you right now because you're the worst. It's bad, Gilbert."

Can I hug her? Is that acceptable? She might claw my face. If I stand up, she'll probably stop talking, and I want her to be able to say everything. It seems she's been holding in so many things. *Lord, let her sift through the lies and find Your truth.*

Another gulping breath and she starts again. "Then Diana and Nathan are so utterly perfect it's maddening. Diana said my online dating profile sucks. What does she know? She's never looked at anyone's dating profile. And Nathan. Nathan! The man was *nice* tonight, and I love him for it because I've always thought he was simply wonderful."

"You're in love with Nathan?"

"Ew! Gilbert." She stretches her arms to the middle of the table and rests her forehead on the wood. "Keep up! I'm in love with what I don't have. I want what Diana has." Her head pops up, and she spears me with a glare. "I don't want six kids and to be a froufrou housekeeper or—I don't know. Maybe I do! Maybe I'd be the best stinking trophy wife you'd ever have!"

Cordelia launches from her chair so fast it falls to the floor. She squeaks and quickly rights it. "I'm sorry. I'm sorry, Gilbert. I don't—" With head tilted to the ceiling, she scrubs her hands over her face. "My brain and my mouth are like these dueling tornados. I don't want to be saying any of this. Especially to you when you're nice and talented and loved by all. You already think I'm unhinged or crazy or whatever. Just like everybody else."

Her arms fling wide, words tumbling down a mountain, an avalanche that has been on the brink for far too long. "You know how many times I've heard that in my life? Cordy, you're crazy! Cordy, you're out of control. Cordy, calm down. Grow up! Settle down. Sit still. Be quiet. Pay attention. What were you thinking?" Her red socks hardly make a sound when she stomps. "I'll tell you! I'm thinking— I'm thinking everything all the time."

She snatches her mug and holds it against her chest with two hands. "Shaun used to say, 'What's going on in that brain?' And..." True vulnerability shines through her expression, and she rubs a finger along her lips. "Was it me? Do you think maybe it's because he thought I was broken? Like, maybe I made him feel... like he needed—He'd say it like he was surprised, but then it wasn't a compliment. But that's not my fault. Is it? Is it bad that I have all these different ideas—if he didn't want to be with me because I was—Ahh." She walks in a small circle clutching her head. "Ignore all of this. I'm sorry, Gil. I get it. I'm a huge disappointment to everyone who knows me. I understand if you don't want to hang out anymore."

I definitely want to hang out more. She never would've dumped any of it unless she felt safe—unless she trusted, in some small way, for me to accept it. Accept her. If I leave now she'll regret it for a really long time. Maybe forever. I set the cards aside and orient my body to her. "Tell me the rest."

"Psh. 'The rest,' he says. Like you haven't heard enough. I need to get through Christmas, and it'll be fine. Everything will be fine. Sometimes I feel trapped by all those people and I get the feeling they hate me."

"Do they?"

"Of course not. Probably not. That'd be dumb." The avalanche has slowed and the last pebbles settle at the foot of the mountain. Her posture slumps.

"If it's worth anything, I'll be here. Right next door. Text me anytime."

"You'll get sick of me." The girl has the audacity to roll her eyes. "I'll be like an itch you can't scratch."

"Try me." I'd like to hear more about this Shaun idiot. But not tonight. "Cordelia. You—Do you hear me? You are not a disappointment. You have a wonderful brain, and you don't need to apologize for it—especially not to me."

"Okay, well." Her gaze flits around the room, unable to land. "You're just saying that because you don't want to be rude. So, thanks for the tea or whatever. You can go now. I have some stuff I gotta do online."

Wait. Online? Did she say an online dating profile? "Or." I raise my hand. "Hear me out. Starting computer work this late might not be the best use of your time. Is there a card game *you* like to play that you can teach me?"

Her legs collapse, and she sits in the middle of the kitchen floor. "I'm tired."

"Sure. Of course. If I leave, will you go to bed?"

She's standing again. "No." Then with a wet rag in hand, she crawls across the floor, mopping. "I can play Speed. You know that one?"

I cross the two steps and force her to stand. She allows me to take the rag and toss it into the sink. Wild red waves dance around her face. "Five cards facedown on either side, keep five in your hand, play up or down in the middle until your personal stack is gone?"

We blink at each other.

Somewhere in the bathroom a faucet drips.

She nods.

The urge to pull her into a hug is strong enough that I physically fight it. If I follow that impulse, there won't be any card games. I'd hug her, for sure. Then I might lose my mind and rub a hand along her back. The girly scent of her shampoo doesn't help matters. If I brushed my hand across her temple and tucked the wayward strands behind her ears, how would I walk away? Provided she reciprocates this feeling even a little, there wouldn't be an easy retreat. And if she does not—

Two friends drinking tea and playing cards. Nothing else.

I think of all the work waiting next door. I'm penniless. I'm not dating. I cannot support a family. I have nothing of value to offer. Therefore, there is no reason for a girlfriend. A girlfriend wants things from me I can't give. She'll want my time. She'll want things I can't buy. She'll demand more of me than I have and when she figures out I won't change for her, she'll leave.

Which is why I am a friend. A friend who enjoys the smell of girly shampoo and wants to replay the part where her hand was in mine.

Write music. Mud drywall. Schedule gigs. Purchase lumber. The beat of these thoughts cools my blood. Construction. Music. Sawdust. Cold showers in unfinished houses.

I retreat one step, then another, until I'm safely in my uncomfortable wooden chair.

I split the deck. Clear my throat. "We'll play for thirty minutes. And then you sleep. Tomorrow, you need to take it easy. Sleep in if you can."

"I don't need your advice, Gilly-boy." She pulls her curls into a bun that flops to the side of her head.

Wow, she's cute. I chuckle on an exhale as I deal the cards. Thirty minutes, then I'm out of here before I act on impulses that would initiate the prelude of losing her forever.

GILBERT

THURSDAY, DECEMBER 21

BON JOVI—IT'S MY LIFE

"Run it again." John fiddles with the sound board, then counts the beat with his fingers, mouthing: *One, two, three, four.* Foam egg crates line the walls and ceiling of the home studio he built in his attic. He sits at his keyboard worth more than my truck.

We're working through our set for tomorrow's show at Westroads Mall in Omaha. They requested "edgy and upbeat but still classical Christmas," so we're adding a new arrangement for this show. I've written a fantasia with strains of "O Come, O Come, Emmanuel" that blends into "Silent Night" and finishes with "Hark the Herald Angel Sings." Touches of "Joy to the World" sprinkle throughout the fifteen-minute piece. If John Williams wrote a sacred track for a pageant, this would be it.

I love that this piece speaks the whole message of the Bible. For background music, it's peaceful but won't knock anyone to sleep. I left plenty of the traditional melodies so listeners will catch a phrase here and there that they'll recognize. It almost feels like cheating to use all these public domain songs.

John records our practice session to upload to YouTube once we have a perfect full set. He promises this will make us money. I don't argue. If he wants to waste the time messing with it, it doesn't make any difference on my end. Dreams don't pay bills.

"Cut." John tosses his headphones to the card table. "That was great. Depending on the crowd, we can play it through twice. Or open with it and recycle it toward the end. Few people shop the whole night, and there's enough variance they'll never know."

"We won't need to." I stand and stretch my arms. "With our regular Christmas set, and now this one, we can easily fill the three hours. You told him we take a fifteen halfway?"

John nods while absently tapping a pencil on his knee. "You going to Aunt J's tonight?"

I frown. John knows I'm always at her Thursday get-togethers.

John doesn't look at me. "I was thinking of asking CJ if she'd like me to pick her up."

"Like a date?"

"I've been trying to connect with her since our original date was canceled." He shrugs. "I guess she's been busy."

"Yeah, she's got a tight deadline for work." What I don't mention is that she texts multiple times a day, delivers me home-cooked food, and I know she doesn't work around the clock because she's had dinner in town with Diana three times this week.

Then there was last night. I stayed for countless rounds of Speed until we were both laughing and exhausted. Only then did we remember the showerhead. That ate up another half-hour. By then we'd stayed up so late our stomachs were growling, and she started bringing out food.

John's expression is hopeful. "Maybe she wouldn't mind if I picked her up."

I rub the back of my neck. "We were going to drive together."

He stands as if he's just remembered something then sits again. "That makes sense. Sure. Yeah. Since you live on the same property." He nods while shuffling sheet music on the piano. "You've not changed your social status. So..."

"Huh?"

"You're not dating. You and CJ aren't—something?"

"Nah, man. Just friends."

"Right. Didn't want to step on anyone's toes."

"Her project is due tomorrow. I'm sure she'd love to spend time with you after Christmas." Why are these words slimy on my tongue? I lean forward and loosen the screw on my cello's endpin.

"Do you have the set list saved from our last gig?" Dating conversation closed.

"I'll email the updated set." Endpin pushed inside the body, I lay my cello in its red-velvet-lined case. "What should we name the long one?"

John pulls out his phone then jumps to his feet. "Yes!" He pumps a fist. "Gil! Yes!"

I look at the screen over his shoulder. There's an email from... I squint but can't read the small text. "What is it?"

"This is the music supervisor I told you about. The Hollywood scout. She heard us play at the cattlemen's banquet back in October. She says she likes what she sees on our website." He gapes with either terror or elation. "She wants us to come to L.A."

"When?"

He glances at his phone. "This weekend."

"Christmas Eve is Sunday."

"She wants to hear us in the studio on the twenty-third. Saturday afternoon."

"Wow. That's—wow." This is huge. Blow-up-our-career huge.

"There's more." John's focus flits along his screen, and I slowly lower myself to the stool. "Okay, here's the catch... she's invited three other groups. We each have... a half-hour slot. It's an audition. She'll have us perform for the producers who will make the final decisions."

"What are we supposed to play?" We want to do this, right? We're a band that plays music for money. People hire us. This is good. Why do I need to convince myself this is good? Of course this is good. It's so far away. Who's paying for the flights? Can we find a place to stay at such short notice? Hotels are outrageous—

"They're filming a new TV drama. Contemporary but with an old-fashioned flare. They're pulling together some of the great entertainment styles from the 1800s in a modern story."

I feel a glimmer of excitement as he continues to read to himself. That could be fun. As long as I don't think about the city. We'd be in a studio. Studios are fine.

"Ha! It's an eight-episode miniseries of a contemporary *Pride and Prejudice*." He lowers his phone. "That's why she wants us. She says we have the perfect blend of traditional and contemporary sounds."

This is true. "So... what are we supposed to play?"

He sucks in a deep breath and tucks his phone in his pocket. "She wants us—that means you—to compose an original mash-up of Handel and something modern. She mentions Michael Jackson or—"

"Jackson's not modern. How old is this chick?"

"He's more modern than Handel. But she also mentions Avicii or Black Eyed Peas."

I nod. "Mash Handel with anything from the last fifty years that makes people move." My knee's nervous energy bumps the nearby card table.

We stare at each other. Our answer is yes. Despite my doubts, this is still the coolest thing that's ever happened to us. It's for star-wishers and the lucky few. Never in my life did I dream an honest-to-goodness Hollywood scout would hear me play and then contact me.

Reality slams like a gut-punch. "That's a lot to put together in two days."

John puffs his chest. "But you can do it."

Can I do it? "I can do it." *Lord, help me.*

He seesaws his shoulders and raises his fists. John makes a better musician than a dancer. He aims at me with double finger guns. "And you will do it."

"I will do it." I run a hand through my hair. "John, you're amazing. Have I expressed how amazing you are? You're amazing. She found us on your website?"

"Oh!" He stops his awkward celebratory dance. "Look who's finally interested in my *hobby*. The website that you never pay any attention to gets 10,000 hits a month. And these are new hits that direct people to and from our YouTube page that currently sits with 3,000 subscribers. Yes, that website."

"I am unworthy." I fall to my knees in a *Wayne's World* bow.

He flicks both hands into the air to conduct an imaginary orchestra and shouts in an indiscernible foreign accent, "From ze top!"

"The top of what? We don't have an arrangement." My

hair will be thinner by the end of this weekend from how many times I've pulled my hands through it.

"True. True." John gathers his music from the piano. "Practice is over. This is good enough for Omaha. My boy has a symphony to write." He pulls a notebook from his backpack and dumps it on what we call my scratch table next to the piano. "This is where you shine, my friend. I'll bring food." He's halfway through the door when he points at me. "You are not to leave this room. I'll be back in two hours. Let's see what you can do by then."

I'm anxious. I usually create our arrangements at my own whims, not on command. Can I create when told? Can I make art for someone else per their preferences? *Lord, work through me.* I stretch my neck side to side with the release of a deep breath.

John bursts into the room with a hand on the door. "Don't overthink this. They're asking because they liked what they heard. Write what feels good. What feels right. Sure, you want to make them happy, but they wouldn't have picked us if they didn't want your stamp."

I only nod and slip on the headphones. I don't need to hear the original songs from her email. I know enough to go for it.

John opens the door again. "You don't have to use Handel." He threads his fingers. "Classical and Pop have a baby."

"John. I got this. Go away."

"I'm going. You've got this."

I wait a measure to see if he's coming back. He doesn't, and I adjust the headphones.

Designs instead of notes take shape on my page. I let my ideas for the arrangement flow like a brain dump. There are no bad ideas at this stage. Sometimes I open a door and decide that's not the hallway I wanted to enter, but I refuse to let myself become discouraged. I simply open another door. I move between my scratch table, piano, and cello. I sit for at least ten minutes on the box drum working out a rhythm and stare across the room without seeing.

Bing!

The interruption sends a flair of annoyance through me. I usually have my phone off during recording sessions and the few times I forget aren't a problem because I don't have that many friends.

Bing!

I throw my pencil across the room where I left my phone at the card table.

Bing!

Before Cordelia I didn't get many texts. Since Cordelia... I feel the tug of a smile. Nobody else in my contacts would send three in a row.

Bing! Make that four.

Bing! Definitely her. I dutifully ignore the allegretto thrum of my heart. Standing, I lean my elbows on the table and glance at the door before scanning the screen.

> Cordelia: There's a guy with a black car at your house.
>
> Cordelia: He's standing outside your door and knocking.
>
> Cordelia: Still knocking.
>
> Cordelia: Ew! He's looking in the windows! Who does that?
>
> Cordelia: Ack, he's walking this way.
>
> Cordelia: I'm not here! I'm hiding.

Cordelia: I don't think he saw me. Gosh, I hope he didn't see me.

Gilbert: Did you lock the door?

Cordelia: Dearest Gilbert. I'm ASTOUNDED at your lack of faith in my "I'm not home" knowhow.

Gilbert: What if he's coming for the eggnog pie?

Cordelia: You ate the rest of it last night. I was going to make you another one, but I forgot. You want another one?

Gilbert: I do love a good eggnog pie.

Cordelia: HE'S COMING OVER HERE!

Gilbert: He must know someone's home. Did you stash the car?

Cordelia: I don't have time for your prattle. You'd prattle all day long if someone didn't put a stop to your nonsense. What does this look like to you? Chitchat around the water cooler? Swapping stories around the campfire??? We have a SITUATION. I'm telling you there's a strange man here that I've never seen before and it's sus. SUS I tell you.

Gilbert: What's your plan?

Cordelia: Text you, obv, and hide.

Gilbert: I'm not home.

Cordelia: OMG GILBERT IF YOU WERE HOME YOU'D DEAL WITH THIS AND I WOULDN'T BE TEXTING YOU.

Gilbert: Together now: Deep breath in.

Cordelia: *GIF of Repunzel hiding in a pyramid of her own hair.*

Gilbert: Does he have a John Travolta look to him? From Grease?

Cordelia: I've never seen Grease.

Gilbert: WHAT?!

Cordelia: DON'T YELL AT ME.

Cordelia: My parents wouldn't let me! And then when I was older I forgot about it.

Gilbert: Stained jeans, black leather jacket, he should wear a hat to keep his ears from freezing off but it would mess up his perfectly styled black hair?

Cordelia: DO YOU HAVE A CAMERA HERE?

Gilbert: It's my brother, Cameron.

Gilbert: He's mostly harmless.

Gilbert: He told me he was coming. I told him it was a recording day, so he'll turn up at Aunt J's eventually.

Cordelia: YOU'RE RECORDING? DID I RUIN YOUR SET?? ARE YOU PLAYING ANYTHING COOL?

Gilbert: Caps are still on, Champ. You can stop yelling.

Gilbert: We were, but I'm composing instead. Or was, before your very important situation.

Gilbert: I only deal with the most important situations during recording sessions.

Cordelia: Puh-lease. Quit being dramatic, Gilly-boy.

Cordelia: Sooo... should I say hi or something? Invite him in?

Gilbert: Gross, no. Keep hiding!! He's nosy but not industrious. He'll call me when he can't get in.

Cordelia: HE'S KNOCKING ON MY DOOR. WHAT DO I DOOO?

Gilbert: You could escape from the back window and take cover in the trees by the field.

Cordelia: *GIF of Michael Bluth from Arrested Development: "Yeah. That makes sense."*

Gilbert: Naw, better not. If he walks around the house to spy in your window, he's bound to notice your footprints in the snow and follow you.

Gilbert: There'll be no hope for you then.

Gilbert: *GIF of Spiderman scaling a building*

Cordelia: *GIF of Peter Parker: "Why is this happening to me?"*

Gilbert: Cordy-girl, since when are you scared to meet new people? SMH

Cordelia: Just a feeling I had. I like to meet people on my own terms.

Cordelia: AND…

Gilbert: And… !!

Cordelia: And I'm in my pajamas and my
hair is wet. You told me to take it easy
today and I'm trying. (So this is your fault.)
My fuzzy pink robe does not match my hair
and that would be a terrible way to meet
someone for the first time.

Gilbert: Oh, wow. You have to match your
clothes to your hair?

Cordelia: I don't HAVE to do anything. But
yes… sort of I do.

Gilbert: You've looked very matchy every
time I've seen you.

Gilbert: That green hoodie might be my
favorite.

Cordelia: Thanks! Can't go wrong with
that one.

Gilbert: He gone yet?

Codelia: IDK. Should I check?

Gilbert: You do you, boo.

Cordelia: Don't ever say that again.

Gilbert: Noted.

Gilbert: I thought I'd try it, but it's not a
good one for me.

Cordelia: Is it for anyone? I feel like
it's not…

Gilbert: Tell me more. You sound torn.

Cordelia: Yes, Mr. Therapist. But do you know what I mean? How people type random epithets with ever so many !!! and for all we know, on the other end of the screen they're BORED OUT OF THEIR EVER-LOVING MIND. Their thumbs are tap tap tap and their heart's not in it. "You do you, boo!"

Gilbert: Girl, I'm dead!!!! AHAHAHAHAHAHA

Cordelia: See! Now I believe nothing. You're actually stuffing your face with lame cellist food wishing I'd stop talking.

Gilbert: That is my food of choice. You are all-knowing.

Cordelia: Maybe this is a girl problem? Where my homies at? Can I say homies? Is that still a thing?

Gilbert: Define homies and I'll let you know... girl.

Gilbert: Heyo! Cam's calling. I'll lure him away.

Cordelia: Lands to the living! You could have literally done that any time.

Cordelia: Let me know when it's safe to spy from my window again.

23

CORDELIA

STRAIGHT NO CHASER—12 DAYS OF CHRISTMAS

"I can't get over these cozy feelings. *Christmas Comforts.* I need to see this collection in print." Gilbert stands the cello case on its end and takes a pie from me as I climb out of the driver's seat of his truck.

"Well get in line, Mister." I reach for the pie but he lifts it away.

"I got it." We avoid the iced over side-walk and crunch along the snow in the yard to Aunt Jewels' front door. "I don't think I can wait until next fall. Wow. I'm stoked for you. And you finished a day early! We should celebrate or something."

"We could go to a party."

"How about tonight?"

"Yes!" I clap my green mittens. "I'll bring pie."

"I'll supply a little music."

"Whoop-whoop!"

Gilbert nudges my shoulder with his elbow and beams a huge smile when we pause on the porch. "Really though, this is a big deal, Cordelia. I'm super proud of you. Can I preorder copies yet? I need ten sets. Minimum. I'll plan to hoard them for a few years then sell them off for my retirement. You'll be rich and famous, and I'll be the old man in a rocking chair reading about you in *Times Magazine*, 'I knew her when—'"

"*Know* her. Good grief. When I'm rich and famous you can brag that you *know* her."

Aunt Jewels swings open her front door. I squeak and reroute my hand that was stretched forward to knock. The joy emanating from her brightens the night as she ushers us into her home. "Opa! Mazel tov! Feliz Navidad." She's sporting forest-green soft overalls with a cream long-sleeved shirt. Her freshly permed white curls sparkle with gold snowflake pins, and her red tennis shoes jingle with each step from bells tied into the laces. A string of red and white felted pom poms loops around her neck.

Gilbert laughs. I laugh because he laughs. I love that he never seems to tamp down his merriment. Aunt Jewels is hilarious, and he doesn't hide his reaction. The way he appreciates his aunt's fun outfits makes me wish I was dressed as brightly. I want to be Aunt Jewels when I grow up.

She taps her toes until all the bells dance and then laughs with us. "Get inside, you two. You're letting out the bought air."

Once we're in, her strong arms squeeze me. The hugs from this small-boned woman have made the list of my top three favorite things in the whole wide world. I'm not sure how I made it twenty-eight years without them.

Her hands grasp my face, and my cheeks are squished against my smile. "How are you, hon?"

Before I can give a cordial response I'm choked with

the burn that precedes tears. *Gah.* Why do her simple questions bring out the waterworks in me? She has this way about her that makes me feel like I'm her absolute favorite. But how could I possibly be her favorite? She's known me for a week. This is only the second time I've been in her home. Yet the acceptance is real. She isn't asking a flippant question. This isn't, "Hey, think we'll get more snow tomorrow?" This is, "Cordelia Jane Thompson, favored niece, daughter of my heart, are you okay? Are you thriving? Are you hurting? Are you well?" And I want to tell her everything because she *sees* me. If I were to expose my darkest sin in this moment, I know in my soul that she would kiss my forehead and tell me that she loves me—and then she'd do whatever it takes to help me crawl back into the light.

Gilbert clears his throat, and she releases my face. "Cordelia finished her cookbook. I'm taking preorders tonight. Tell all your friends."

I roll my eyes, but the smile I try so hard to suppress strains my muscles.

"Put me down for two." Her soft hand pats my face. "We'll talk soon," she promises. She greets Gilbert in a similar manner, though she kisses his cheeks instead of squishing them.

"I'll try not to miss dinner. Would it be possible if I used your office? I need your printer." He tries to squeeze past her in the entry. This is difficult with his cello between us.

"Oh." I put a hand on his arm. "You should have said something. I have a printer set up at the cottage."

"Thanks, Cordelia. I'll remember that next time." He flashes a grin that has me chanting to myself that we're just friends. *We're neighbors and friends and that's it!* My traitorous feelings are trying to build castles on sand.

Aunt Jewels takes the pie dish from his hand and waves him off.

An incoming text vibrates my pocket. I should turn off my phone for the evening because I'm sick of living in two separate worlds. All of the many *many* wheel-turning rodents in my mind need to be banished. There's an especially large wheel hogging way too much space regarding the smidge of regret that I agreed to meet David K. for coffee tomorrow. I wasn't a complete imbecile though. I timed the date so I can fetch Mark from the airport afterward. This provides a fantastic escape if we don't connect. Based on our previous few conversations, I have zero excitement regarding his latest message flashing across the screen.

> David: I'm looking forward to meeting you tomorrow.

I plop onto the middle of the couch in the unoccupied living room.

> Cordelia: Me too.

I click off the screen, but before I put the phone away he responds.

Bing!

> David: It's cool to make a connection with someone so quickly. I hope it goes well at the coffee shop.

He thinks we have a connection? Mark's ominous warnings haunt me. *Shush!* What does Mark know? Okay, so David is not very exciting through a text conversation and an in-person date is the most efficient way to discover for sure if we click. If the date is a bust we'll never speak again, and I'll move to another plan.

Plan G. I snicker at my clever coding. *No, CJ, Plan G is already a bust.* The man has had ample opportunity to make a move and he has not. Except... why does it feel wrong to go out with David?

I refuse to feel guilty for planning dates. Even if my traitorous heart is preoccupied. I'll wait for Anne Shirley's Gilbert. The one who wants to be with me, who's pining for me—the one who'll stand by me through my silly escapades. And while I wait there's no harm in practicing my new serious and focused demeanor.

Ha! That's what this is. Practice. Practice dates. I can practice being CJ. Someone who is just a little—a lot—more serious. A little better at sitting still. Maybe someone that a man in a suit might like to hang on his arm. I can do better. I can try harder. I can be normal.

> Cordelia: I'll order a white chocolate peppermint latte. It'll guarantee at least one of us has a good time.

> David: Oh, I meant that I hope our date goes well.

My thumbs have betrayed me! They hesitate over the two-inch keyboard.

> Cordelia: Yeah, sorry. I was making a joke. I promise I'm cool. But it's only a first date. Let's not get too worked up.

> David: I'm a regular coffee guy. I don't usually drink caffeine after lunch, so I'm not sure what I'll order.

> Cordelia: Okay.

> Cordelia: Hey, I don't mean to shut you down, but I'm kind of at a thing right now and need to put my phone away.

> David: Oh! Okay. Bye.

> David: What kind of a thing? Like a Christmas party?

> David: Where did you say you lived?

I didn't. I didn't say where I lived, because it would be creepy to even tell him what town. He could drive into Hadley Springs and ask anyone where I live, and they'd give out directions.

The screen eventually goes black when I don't answer, and I'm left staring at my phone's dim reflection of the Christmas tree. I met my last deadline for work. I'm allowed to celebrate. I should be excited. One afternoon out of town. One date.

"Hi. I'm Cameron."

My gaze follows the outstretched hand in front of me to dark hair, styled dramatically in a swoop across his forehead, thickly knit beige sweater and jeans. I place my hand in his. "Hi. I'm Cordelia. CJ. People call me CJ." His hand is soft. Not at all like Gilbert's.

Which isn't relevant in any way. Of course.

"May I sit?" He sits beside me without waiting for an answer.

"You're Gilbert's brother, right?" I scooch to give him more space on the couch.

The room is beginning to fill, and it's louder with more guests arriving with food. The couch seems to burn him, because he immediately jumps to his feet and waves across the room. "Hey, John! C'mere." He sinks onto the couch again, our shoulders brushing. "I was real mad when I heard he rented the cottage to someone else. But I get it now."

"What?" Does Cameron think I did something to weasel my way into the cottage? "Did you want to rent it?"

"It makes sense. You're 100% his type. You know the saying, though it's never true. Bros before—"

"What's up?" John's eyebrows are raised in question once he reaches us.

"What do you think about Gil moving into the big house?" Cameron gestures to me before he drums his fingers on his knee.

"Nope." John raises his hands. "Do not come crying to me with your family drama."

"But John, you know I've been asking him to let me live there. Begging for months to let me stay with him. First he told me there wasn't room. Then told me the big house wasn't livable. Then he rents to her? A tiny girl woman?" He glances at me. "No offense."

"Um." I speak slowly. "Offense taken."

John runs a hand down his face. "Cam, you gotta stop picking fights in public."

Cameron crosses his arms like a grumpy adolescent. "It doesn't make sense."

"It does. CJ has a job. It pays her this green paper stuff. She can use these papers to purchase things of her own. Like renting a—"

"I'm his brother."

John looks at me apologetically and cuts back to Cameron. "CJ's paying rent. Get over it."

"It's a low-blow if you ask me." He huffs out a breath and shakes his hands in front of him as if flinging drops of water. "Whatever. What's Hadley Strings playing tonight?

185

Anything new? I heard about the L.A. gig. That's cool, I guess."

"Thanks, I guess." John tucks his hands in his pockets. He directs a smile at me, as if I'm in on the news.

"It's about time you broke out of this lousy town. I don't think Gil has the guts to do it though. He'll be eaten alive." Cameron blows a raspberry with a thumbs down gesture. "He's too nice."

"What L.A. gig?" I've decided Cameron is perhaps my least favorite person, even if he has information that interests me.

Cameron swings toward me, his green eyes so similar to Gilbert's it's disorienting. "The duo wiggled into a Hollywood audition. It's all over town." His voice goes flat.

I glance at John for confirmation. The scowl on John's face doesn't match the news.

"And we're all very excited and don't need your energy-sucking negativity about it just because you're jealous." John offers me his hand. "You want something to drink?" He jerks his head toward the kitchen, almost pleading for me to get up and follow him.

"Absolutely. I'm parched." I take John's hand, and he pulls me from the couch. When I stand he doesn't drop it right away but tows me through the living room. I catch Diana's gaze in the entryway as she's helping remove Lisa's coat. She cocks her head and asks in sister-code: *Why is John holding your hand? Did you give up on your online dating profile? I thought for sure you wanted to hold Gilbert's hand.*

I answer with a shrug: *Beats me, sis! It's awkward for sure, but I don't want to hurt anybody's feelings. I'll check back in a few minutes.* And then John pulls me around the corner into the hallway.

John takes us halfway down the hall to the bedrooms

before he stops, and I bonk my face into his back. Still holding my hand by the way.

"Hey." He's out of breath. More so than someone who's only skedaddled across the house. "Sorry. I shouldn't've run my mouth. Cameron is—doesn't usually—he's just—Cameron is Cameron. Don't let him get to you. He doesn't mean any harm."

"Okay. Thank you?" I glance over my shoulder where the guests crowd the living room and back at my hand still in his. "It's—"

"Would you want to have dinner with me?" John smiles.

"Oh." That. I should have seen that coming since our previous evening was canceled. Here I was hoping he'd lost interest. Especially since I never found it. The interest, I mean. "I can't. I don't think—It's like this. I have a date tomorrow. Nothing serious."

"Too serious to grab a pizza?"

"I like pizza." Why can't I like John? I don't know John enough not to like John. He's really nice. Why is there chemistry with some people and absolutely nothing with others? Maybe John would share a pizza with a group of friends. "I can't commit to a time right now—"

"Secret club meeting?" Gilbert's voice beside my ear sends a zap of electricity through my heart.

"Arrgh!" Mid-gasp, I jump-turn and strike his shoulder with a pitiful karate chop. "Where did you come from?"

"Office." He pokes my waist and my karate hands shield my side. "Can I be in the secret club?" While biting the tip of his tongue, he pokes the unprotected ribs on my other side. "Please." He laughs when I strike him again.

Poke. Strike. Giggle. Poke. Strike.

"Hya!" I attempt an offensive maneuver before he pokes again. He nabs my wrists and spins me around until my back is pressed into his chest. With his chin resting on the top of my head, he secures my arms crossed over my chest. The fact remains that grown-up boys are very strong. *Mmm*, and warm. His arms cocoon me, and I relax against his broad chest, clearly beaten. What's a girl to do?

"I've captured you," he whispers.

His voice sends a delightful shiver along my spine.

And there's John. No longer smiling.

24

GILBERT

LOVERBOY—WORKING FOR THE WEEKEND

John crosses his arms, and I can tell by the way he lifts his chin that he's about to word vomit. Not sure what I did. Not sure that I care with Cordelia relaxed against my chest. She angles her face to mine. "John and I were planning a pizza party. Wanna come?"

"Gilbert has to work." John twitches an eyebrow that says everything else to me. *Right, buddy? Not dating because of all the work you have to do? But you're flirting like a teenager. Make up your mind, because you're being a tool.*

"Hey guys." Cameron saunters down the hall. "She's paying rent, huh?"

Since Cordelia offers no resistance to the hold I put her in, at this point I'm giving her a hug. We're hugging. The kind of hug by two people who are dating and familiar with the casual touch of each other.

She steps aside the same moment I drop her wrists and clear my throat.

"I have to work." I nod like a bobble head. "Uh, big

189

project. John, you'll have to play without me tonight. I'm—yep, going to head out now and get started. Cam, you meet, um, CJ? This is CJ." *Breathe, Gilbert. Chill. Out.* "Cam, CJ. CJ, Cam. I'll catch you later."

I'm three steps away when I remember she drove us into town. The tan carpet muffles my footsteps as I return. "Sorry." I take Cordelia's elbow. "Can I talk to you?" Without waiting for her answer, I tug her into the office and shut the door.

The room is small. A corner desk and a bookshelf filled with inspirational fiction, biblical studies, and commentaries fill the tiny office. I shove the swivel chair under the desk to make room for the two of us.

"Secret *secret* club meeting?" Cordelia smirks, and I find myself wanting to wipe it off with something too intimate. I can't control my thoughts around her. When did this happen? I need to change this score before it crescendos.

Here I am, the weekend before the biggest chance of my musical career, and I'd rather spend time with some girl than do the work.

This. This is why I don't date! I don't have time for this nonsense. I can't lead her on to expect more from me than I'm able to give. If I act on this feeling, I'll disappoint her, and she'll leave within a month...

Cordelia taps her finger against the side of my face. "What're you thinking?" She's been in the habit of touching me since we met. Brushing sawdust from my shoulders. Fixing my hair. Unbuckling my seatbelt. Every time she touches me, I freeze because I want to swallow her up. I want to drag her to my chest and hold her. Run my fingers into her tangled hair. Kiss her until she has to come up for air.

I step away. "I can't do this." Phone in hand, I unlock

the screen and fiddle with it. Doing nothing but finding something to look at besides her.

"Do what? Pizza party? It's cool. John says you have to work? I wish you'd told me about L.A." She tucks her hands in her hoodie pocket.

"I didn't want to distract you from your own deadline. And I was busy getting the set together. We're booked for the mall tomorrow night, so John got us a room in Omaha and we'll fly out early Saturday. Zip-zip and home again Sunday."

"That sounds awesome. Celebrity band. I wish I could go." A laugh bursts from her, and she claps her hands while bouncing on her toes. "When you're super famous, can I be your traveling chef and paparazzi? Wouldn't that be fun! I could make you food and film your gigs." Her hands form a little camera box pointed toward my face. "John'll manage websites, scheduling. He and I could set up a killer social media plan. Then you write all our new stuff. Dream team for sure. We'd be unstoppable!" She ends her little speech in a Captain Marvel pose, fist to the sky.

Phone camera on, I snap a quick shot of her. "You're a goose."

"Oh." She deflates. Shoulders curve inward. Face points to the floor. "Why did you bring me in here?"

"I'm going home. But I don't want to leave you stranded. John will jump on the chance to drive you home, but I don't want you uncomfortable if you prefer to make plans with your sister. I just needed to touch base without spectators. Give you the chance to make your own decision about it."

"That was thoughtful. I'll talk to Diana."

"Thoughtful would've been letting you drive yourself if I wasn't planning to stay."

"But we checked off another driving lesson. I think I'm getting better."

I chuckle. "At this rate you'll be on your own in five years."

She makes a noise deep in her throat like a buzzer. "Just for that I'm throwing out that last piece of chocolate pie I saved for you." Her pointer finger digs into my chest.

I remove her hand but keep it in mine. "What? No! I take it back." The physical points of contact between our hands warms my whole arm until I feel it in my stomach.

"Yes, sir. I won't eat it because I'm getting fat on pie. In the trash it goes. So sad for you."

When I lean forward to poke her in the side, she jerks her hand back and hops out of the way.

A quick rap on the door has me crossing my arms and leaning against the desk as Diana enters. "There you are." She shoots me a disapproving glance and hikes Jack on her hip. "I've been looking all over for you. Not you." Her hand waves a dismissal my direction. "You. Can you watch the kids Friday? Tomorrow? Nathan said he'd take me out for once in my life now that you're here."

"All six?" I interrupt.

"No, just the cat." Diana huffs. "Yes, all six. But mostly the twins and Lisa. Lauren can manage Jack, and you won't hear a peep from Landon."

Cordelia shrugs. "Can't tomorrow, but what about Saturday?"

"Or you watch them tomorrow and Nathan and I pick up Mark instead while we're in the city."

"Can't. I have a date."

"With who?" Diana and I speak together.

Cordelia straightens her shoulders. "With *whom* is nunya." Her smile turns mischievous, and she wiggles her eyebrows. "Haha. Kidding. C'mere baby." Jack leans for her, and Cordelia snuggles him. "David K., the home inspector. Should be riveting. Do you think Nathan would let me borrow one of his sweaters?"

I've heard enough. She has a ride home. I printed the music sheets for the song I'm almost finished with. John's right. I can't stay.

"See you girls later."

They barely pause their discussion to acknowledge my exit.

25

CORDELIA

FAITH HILL—WHERE ARE YOU CHRISTMAS?

At the click of the door, Diana swoops in for the kill. "Just what do you think you're doing in here? Closeted up alone? Sometimes I don't understand you at all. You know better than this."

"Secret secret club meeting. Stop hassling. We're just friends."

"You can't do that. You can't put yourself in situations like this."

"Why not? You're always two feet away. Nothing's going to happen." This is my office now and I pull out the spinny chair. "He doesn't even like me."

"Stop it. That's not the point."

"Then what's the point? You trust me to babysit but not take care of myself?"

"Yeah, kinda."

"Oh, good grief." I consider telling her we slept together, but I'm not a monster. "What's your problem?" I spin my chair in a circle so I can stick my tongue out.

"My problem is that you should know better. It's highly inappropriate to be alone with a man who's not your husband. Period. The end. It's a simple rule that will keep you safe from harm, from accusations and misunderstandings. It's just—just quit thinking you're the exception."

"Ok. You done?"

"Yes. So, Saturday? You and Mark could put the kids to bed while we go out?"

"Sure. I need a ride home tonight. Don't leave me."

"Got it."

"What are the chances of Jack making a mess on my shirt in the next half-hour?"

"Twenty-thirty odds."

"Like sixty percent?"

"He either will or he won't. Take this." Diana drapes a burp cloth over my shoulder.

"Go away." I pat his face with the cloth. "I'm going to stew in here with Jack until I'm not mad at you anymore."

"All right. I love you."

"Yep."

Jack offers an open-mouthed smile when I sit with him and clear drool spills from his mouth. Four white teeth peek along his bottom gum and two on the top. I run my finger along the row of new baby teeth, and he chomps my finger. I squeak in pain, and it startles him so he cries.

"Oh, Jack, Jack, Jack," I croon.

Huge drops of tears pour from his baby blues before he pulls it together.

"Sorry, dude. That was totally my bad. You have every right to bite the finger in your mouth." I sit him up on my knee and bounce him while chanting. "You—can bite—the fing—ger in—your mouth." Giggles erupt because I am the funniest thing he's ever seen. "Yesssir. Now listen, little man. When you grow up to be big and strong like Aunt Cordy, keep it together. Figure out what you want, and go for it. Don't wait around. Wasting time. The time is now! Got it? You jiggin' with me?"

His round cheeks are like pillows. Smile relaxed, more drool spills out and I wipe it with his own sleeve. "You jiggin' with something. Swallow that, buddy. Swaaall-looowww. People might look at you funny if you keep that up." He stares at me so seriously while waiting for my next joke.

"You like to bounce, don't you? We can bounce. Bounce, bounce, bounce!" His laughter is heart-melting. "I should bring you along on my date. You might scare him off."

I'm over it before I even start. Why am I doing this again? I pull out the phone and show Jack the picture of David. "What do you think? Look like uncle material to you?" I sigh. "Uncles are supposed to be cool. You know who'd make a really cool uncle?"

No. I won't even say it to a baby. No, no, no, no, no! This is torture. Why can't Gilbert like me back?

I'm crushing so hard on my landlord it's unacceptable. The man is amazing. He is so funny, and talented, and he has those muscles, and he's nice. Nice! Ha. He's beyond nice. John is nice. Gilbert Conner is fire-under-my-skin. And that smile. Killin' me.

I'm convinced the only way to get a song that's stuck in your head out of your head, is to find another song. Even that resolution isn't enough to stop my next text.

> Cordelia: Instead of the coffee shop. Want to meet at the mall food court instead? I heard there's going to be live music.

David: Sounds good. More food/drink
options. That could be fun.

And it could be torture.

The office door creaks and I swivel around to see who's intruding this time.

"Oh, good." Aunt Jewels steps inside and shuts the door. "You're alone. Mostly."

"Sorry. Is it okay that I'm in here?"

"Hush. We haven't much time. Gilbert's birthday is next month. I want your help to throw his party."

"Me?"

"You're such good friends, it would be silly not to include you."

"But I hardly know him."

"Rubbish." She pulls a yellow notepad from the shelf and licks the end of a pencil. I don't think you're supposed to do that. "Now, hon. I'll have you get him there, since he'll never suspect. He'll be so distracted this time, we'll surprise him for sure. Golden thirty. Oh, to be thirty again. What a decade that was. We'll have John arrange the food. He can get the trays catered by the grocery no problem. Nickie will spread the word around town. Between the grocery and the clinic, we'll have the whole town. The real trick is getting him to the church. There's no way we can host it here. Too small."

Jack tries to take my earring and I grab his hand. "But are you sure a big party is really what he wants?"

She stops writing and then draws a line across her page. "Oh, my stars. What was I thinking? You're right, you're right! See, now this is why I need your help. I know the boy, but I get so excited about parties I forget who it's for. Dear me, I'm planning the wrong party. Wrong party, indeed.

Heavens to Betsy. Too much attention will run him off. He can play, but don't make him mingle. New plan. Best friends. Small group. We'll have it here after all. You're completely right."

She sings a soprano trill of excitement. "You, me, John, Nickie, Cameron. Cameron should still be here by then. Who else? We'll invite Diana's crew to fill in the gaps. Never good to have too quiet of a party. Too bad his parents are out of the country this whole time. We'll get them on a video chat for a few minutes at least. You know they're working with the refugee missionaries in Germany?" Her pencil trails down the list then she adds another note to her paper.

"I suppose that's easy then. Your job is much the same. Still very important. You're going to need to get him here under false pretenses. Don't lie to the boy. He'll see right through it. We'll think of something. I can't just invite him over or he'll suspect. I want this to be perfect. He deserves to be celebrated. Everyone does, you know. When's your birthday?" She laughs under her breath. "No surprise party for you this year. You'll never suspect the first year." Her intense expression holds mine as she peers at me over her red glasses. "Birthday?"

"Oh, November second."

"Good, good. Now." She sets the notebook aside. "Tell me what's got you locked in this office alone. You're mad at Diana. What else?"

Lands to the living, does this woman never breathe?

"Can I tell you what I think?" She taps the pencil eraser on Jack's head.

I smile with a nod. I won't try to stop her because I don't think it would work anyway.

"I think you're trying to grab life by the throat and make

it listen to you. You want something so badly you're forgetting the One who controls all things. Wait, my darling girl. Go on your date tomorrow. Oh, don't look so surprised, Diana told me all about it. She loves you so much and is only worried about you. Go on your date. Perhaps this David is the man for you. But remember that the Father loves you very much and has great things in store for you. Wait on Him, and let Him show you how much He loves you. Now, hon, don't you cry again. Here, baby. Use Jack's towel for those tears. Everything is going to turn out just fine. Just you wait and see."

CORDELIA

FRIDAY, DECEMBER 22

FOR KING AND COUNTRY—O COME, O COME, EMMANUEL

It took ninety-three minutes to straighten my curls. If that doesn't make me serious I don't know what will. I hate it. It's in my face, and I can't stop messing with it.

David is supposed to meet me here at the mall food court in ten minutes. On one hand this could be the most unromantic date. But then again, sweet high school nostalgic feelings are blooming. Magic can happen in a mall food court.

Practically though, it's public which equals safe. It's bright and loud, so the mood isn't awkward. I'm twenty minutes from the airport so I can pick up Mark without any trouble. There's also a band playing here from six to nine. Hadley Strings. You heard of them? I'm told they're really good...

Minutes drag by while I force myself to stay off my phone. *Dear God, what am I doing here? I am not excited for this at all. Can I leave? I feel so stupid I didn't talk this through with you.*

"Hello. CJ?" A deep voice startles me from my prayers. The cup of water half-way to my mouth doesn't make it and I spill a mess down the front of my shirt. "Oh…"

I meet the surprised expression of a dark haired, olive-skinned man in his mid-thirties. "David?"

"Yeah, are you okay?" He grabs a handful of paper napkins left on the table beside us. "Here."

And we're off to the races. "Thanks." With my foot, I push out the chair across from me. "Have a seat, good sir." Ack! No silly names. *Be cool, Cordy. Be cool.* "How were the roads on your end of town?" That's a good start. Serious and boring questions.

"Just fine. And you?"

"Yep. Roads being roads. Black and gray. Dashes down the middle."

He offers a gentle smile and stares at me. What is he even thinking? I don't like this at all. There should be a list of what we are supposed to do and say. That should be a thing. Maybe it already is a thing and I missed it. Oh, no. What if there's an email I missed from Friendly Fish detailing how to go through your first meet-up? David's probably waiting for me to start the conversation, and I don't know what it is because I missed the email.

Can I search my inbox now? No. There's no way I could get out my phone and not be rude. It's fine. I'll wing it.

I'm CJ Thompson. Food photographer, author, chef. Business woman. Career girl. I'm serious and focused. I mean business. I'm ready to meet the love of my life.

I clear my throat as he sits across from me.

"Nervous?" He hasn't moved his gaze from mine. It's suffocating. I'm drowning. Can't breathe! Why is he so intense?

"Nah." I flick my gaze to the table top, his eyes, his hands that are folded peacefully on the table, the people in line at the smoothie bar behind him, and zip back to his face. More precisely, his left ear. A lock of black hair covers the top of his ear. There's a tiny pierced hole in his earlobe but no earring. Interesting.

He fingers his ear as if he knows I was looking at it. "I'm a little nervous. It's okay."

"Yeah, sure." I breathe. In. Out. "I guess I am too." How do people do this? Do most people look at each other in the face while they're talking? Ahhh!

Breathe normally.

Make eye contact.

Don't be weird.

Can he tell that my breathing isn't normal?

This is worse than when I'm at the doctor's office and he puts the stethoscope on my back. How does he want me to breathe? Is he listening to my lungs and needs a deep breath to see if I'm harboring bacteria-laden fluid, or should I sort of breathe real slow and shallow because the doctor's listening to my heart?

Clammy sweat breaks out down my spine. I had no idea a first date with a stranger would be as much fun as a doctor's visit.

That easy smile adorns his face again. David really is a good-looking guy. "Let's grab something to eat."

He stands up and I don't. He nods toward the row of fast food options and I sit here paralyzed. He sighs, sits back down, drums his fingers on the table between us.

"Have you ever wanted something so badly you forget why you wanted it?" My blurted question hangs over the table between us. "I'm not who you think I am."

"And who do I think you are?" David is straight-faced.

Is he acting facetious? Do I detect a dry sense of humor under there, or is this really him? Blankly asking questions. "Are you not CJ Thompson?"

"My name is Cordelia. Cordelia Jane. I'm her. I'm really very fun and silly. Most of the time. Except for when I'm not. People think I'm a little weird."

"No. You?" Ah. There's the sarcasm. But he delivers it with such ease, one could almost assume he was sincere. "Is there anything else you need to tell me? If you're sure you're not a double agent, I want to discuss this further over a milk-shake."

When I offer nothing he tips his head a tiny fraction of an inch. "Burger and fries? Chicken and rice? Protein smoothie?" David glides his hand in a straight line toward the food options. "What's your pleasure?"

"Food is good." I stand and at that moment there's a pop of a microphone being turned on. At the far end of the food court, John stands next to his piano while Gilbert adjusts his cello between his knees on the stool nearby.

"Happy holidays, everyone." John smiles as if everyone here came to see him. "Thanks for coming out tonight! I know you're all busy with your last-minute shopping. Don't forget to grab something for Great Uncle Dale. I heard he'll be in town this year." A small wave of laughter ripples across the food court. "We're Hadley Strings, a two-man group. I'm John Brader. This gent on the cello is Gilbert Conner. Be sure to check out our YouTube and website. That's Hadley Strings."

Gilbert looks up and smiles at nobody in particular. It's a generic smile. Not the one I'm used to seeing. Still, it settles me. I feel peace wash over me at his familiar presence.

"You want to snag a table closer to the band?" David points to an empty spot near my boys. "Live music is fun."

"Sure."

"Why don't you reserve a table? I'll get the food. What would you like?"

Oh, my heart. David seems like a really nice guy. It's not fair to do this to myself or him. "David. I'm really sorry." I tap my heel repeatedly on the linoleum. "Ah, shoot. This isn't going to work." I hang my head and look at the pointed toes of my boots that are killing my feet right now. "I—"

"You're not over an ex, are you?" He straightens his shoulders when I look at him. Hands tucked in his pockets, eyebrows raised in question.

Shaun's face flitters through my mind. "Oh, Shaun isn't the problem."

"How long were you together?"

"A couple years, but it's—" I nod to Gilbert. Just looking at him, my heart knows where it wants to be. The sweet sounds of their music feels like home. I'd rather be a friend of Gilbert, than a girlfriend of anyone else. "I think I'm in love with the cello man."

"Who?" David spins toward the musicians. His face doesn't harden with jealousy. He's relaxed. Curious. "What's special about him? You know these guys?"

"He's my landlord, actually."

Gilbert closes his eyes while leaning into the melody of "Let it Snow."

David twitches his lips to the side in thought. "Hm. David the home inspector doesn't stand a chance against that. Guess I strike out again. Can we still get dinner? You can tell me all about him over a burger."

"You don't need to do that. I already feel bad enough.

This is a rotten thing to do to a guy—much less on the weekend of Christmas."

"Now you'll send me off hungry as well?"

"Let me get the food then. You reserve a table—sit wherever you like."

"Bacon cheeseburger, please. And a rootbeer."

"That's right, no caffeine after lunch."

He smiles gently. "You remembered."

27

GILBERT

WHITESNAKE—HERE I GO AGAIN

Twenty minutes into our set I spot Cordelia with some guy I've never seen before in khaki pants and a green sweater. I almost didn't recognize her with hair ironed flat as my grandpa's Sunday pants and dark make-up around her eyes. She doesn't look like herself at all. This must be some kind of business meeting. There's no blushing, laughing, or flirting from what I see. I try to ignore them. But my traitorous gaze keeps wandering over to her table.

She catches me watching her once, and she raises a hesitant hand toward me. I smile and turn my attention to my set notes. Does she seem nervous? What kind of business meeting takes place at a food court on a Friday evening?

At the end of the next song it hits me. This is David. The date from her online thing. Well, then. I pity both of them. If that's what dating in the modern world looks like, count me out.

John steps toward me while pretending to straighten my music stand. "Just go talk to her. Your head's not in the game, man." He shoots me a father-like expression. "And let the record state that I bow out. I won't compete with whatever's going on between the two of you."

"I'm not dating—"

"Stuff it. You're not dating. Big whoop. You're completely crushing on each other."

"It's not like—"

"Shut up, we're on." He returns to his keyboard and hammers out the chords to the next song.

"Are you mad?" I catch up by the second measure.

"No."

"You're playing like you're mad."

"I'm mad." We go on together and he picks up the tempo. Normally, I lead the set. Keeping up with John takes all of my focus. Our version of Tchaikovsky's "Dance of the Sugar Plum Fairy" is completed in record time. Out of breath from the effort, he steps toward me again.

I wipe my palm on the back of my shirt and wait for him to speak.

He shuts off my mic and speaks quietly ten inches from my face. "You're a fool if you don't act on this. To have something as special as you and CJ have and pretend it's nothing, it's—it's garbage. Don't waste a good thing."

"You really think she likes me—like that?"

"I've never known you to be an idiot, Gilbert." He straightens. "When we get back from L.A. you're going to do something about this, or I'm—I quit. I'm not going to be in a band with an idiot. I'll find another musical genius. You're replaceable, you know."

I work at controlling my features. Obviously he doesn't mean it. We're not the kind of friends to throw out threats like that. His point was made loud and clear though. Do I believe him?

CHAPTER 27

The first half of our set blows by without more discussion, and I do my best to keep from staring at Cordelia and her date. John's outburst ruminates through my mind song after song. I eventually come to the conclusion that he's not wrong. The snag is my glaring lack of resources. I'm a broke house-flipping musician. And I'm comfortable here.

If we land the job in California, the future of the band would be set. I could quit construction as a business, work on my own projects while enjoying life as a famous cellist in Hollywood.

There's a blur of fantasy edging this daydream. I have no idea what kind of life that would be. How can I tell John that I'd rather stay broke in Hadley Springs, Nebraska?

Halfway through "Last Christmas" I watch Cordelia and her date stand up. She gathers the trash from the table and piles it on the tray. The other man takes the tray from her. They shake hands. He walks toward the trash can. She strides toward the mall exit while zipping her coat.

Why would she wait for me? I have nothing to offer.

28

CORDELIA

SATURDAY, DECEMBER 23

PERRY COMO—SILVER BELLS

Here's the problem: I haven't spoken to Gilbert since Thursday when he pulled me into the office and Diana ran him out. Now I can't get him out of my head. I'm 68% sure he was flirting with me in that hallway. That's not a grade to post on the fridge, but it's passing. It's a clear sign that I need to study before the next test.

I replay the exchange and remember how the sides of his eyes crinkle with his smile and he bites the end of his tongue while trying to poke me. I feel his arms hold me tight. They are solid. Warm. I smell his unique blend of sawdust and aftershave. The zing of pleasure plants a smile on my face. He whispers, "I've captured you," and I'm melting.

Can we be more than friends? Am I more than just some girl he hangs out with because I live next door? Did I misread the signs? Watching him perform at the mall and not be allowed to talk was like baking and photographing an eggnog pie and then being commanded not to eat it. What kind of cruel world is this? I'm Winnie the Pooh sitting under the name of Sanders with his fist knocking against his head. "Think, think, think, think."

I detect a trail of breadcrumbs. It's quite possible Gilbert isn't directly opposed to becoming more than friends. Oh, the uncertainty! I will not be the one to mess this up. I signed a one-year lease. I'm adult enough to be cool. I will not make this weird two weeks into my contract.

I deleted Friendly Fish over burgers with David. His advice actually. "I recommend canceling your subscription if you're going to reject men before dinner. Save yourself the angst. And theirs." Smart fellow, that one. "You tried it. Check it off one of your lists. The man you're after isn't on the app."

David was pretty great all told. He didn't seem upset about the failed date. We talked about this and that and other unimportant things and parted ways. I was perfectly on time to pick up Mark from the airport. We had a delightful drive back to Hadley Springs despite the new snowfall. Then I ended up staying at Diana's last night because I fell asleep on the couch.

Which brings me to my current dilemma. It's six twenty-two a.m. and I have to pee like a mother. Can't do a thing about it because I'm the favorite of all favorite aunts. I'm the Queen of Queens.

Jack and Lisa crowd my lap. Leo and Lance squish into the corner beside me with Landon on the other. My feet are further trapped by Lauren, who sits on the floor leaning against my calves. We're watching the Christmas edition of everyone's favorite baking show.

Shuffles of slippered feet draw my attention to the arched entry of the kitchen. "Morning, family."

"Mark!" A chorus of shouts drown the TV. Leo's elbow

knocks the side of my face when he leaps from the couch. "Mark! Mark, Mark, Mark!" They're like yapping dogs. I'm left with a bruised ego and a whimpering Jack.

"What are you fussing about, baby cakes? You'll get your chance." I hold in my chuckle at Mark's intake of breath. He raises his coffee mug above the mayhem and holds his other hand out protectively.

"Stop." The gremlins immediately obey his command, and I'm torn between a flash of jealousy and wanting to instantly follow his orders myself.

"Line up." They do.

"No, in order of height. No talking." And they do!

"Hmm." He's Captain VonTrapp inspecting the line of children. "Jump three times. Spin in a circle. That's two circles, Lance. Enough. You may give me a high-five but if you spill this coffee on her new carpet, you will make your mother cry and nobody wants that over Christmas." He walks down the line like bejeweled royalty and they gently tap his outstretched hand. "You're going to get dressed as quietly as possible—like sneaky secret agent ninjas—because if you wake your parents our whole day is ruined. Once you're dressed we'll go for a walk to look at the snow... and maybe I'll buy you donuts." He holds a finger to his lips. "On your mark, get set, go!"

Well, there goes my throne. "Here." I lay Jack on the carpet. "Watch this one while I pee."

"Can he have donuts?"

"What?" I turn back in shock.

"Kidding."

I hum inquisitively. I don't think he was kidding. "Just... sit there. I'll be right back."

When I return, Mark is thumbing through my phone with a bemused smile.

"Hey!" I snatch it from him. "Snoop. How'd you know my passcode?"

"I could tell you, but then I'd have to kill you."

"You're the worst." I punch his arm as hard as I can.

"Ow! Coffee! Watch it. It's not my fault you've used the same four numbers since middle school." He taps the side of his head and clicks his tongue.

A text comes through and I look down.

> Gilbert: Hey Champ, can you call me?

I quickly scroll through our conversation and notice he's sent three messages that I hadn't seen yet. Mark must have been reading through days worth of texts between the two of us just now. Unwelcome heat runs up my neck and face. Seeing these innocent words through my cousin's eyes confirms the suspicion that Gilbert and I have most definitely been flirting.

I call Gilbert and straighten my spine. I'm allowed to enjoy the company of a friend. There are no rules I have broken.

"Hey." At that one sweet word from Gilbert, a swirl of anticipation brushes the inside of my stomach. A grin follows, and I turn my back to Mark and amble into the kitchen. Sooo casual. Nothing to see here.

"Is everything okay? Shouldn't you be on a plane?" I pour coffee into a yellow mug and liberally add cream and a scoop of sugar.

"Guess God has other plans. All planes grounded this morning because of the storm."

My heart sinks. "You're going to miss your audition! Can you reschedule? There's no way they can hold this against you. You can't control the weather. They have to know it's not your fault. Can you get in touch with them right way?"

"Relax." He sounds extremely calm over this, and I feel like I need to be double upset for him. "It wasn't meant to be."

"No, no, no. You can still figure this out. It's just a minor difficulty."

"God doesn't make things difficult. When he closes a door. He closes it. This is what we needed. I was up most the night asking if this was the right thing—for God to make the answer clear. I know it's right because when I got the alert from the airport that the flights were canceled—Cordelia, I had the best feeling about it. I sighed in relief and fell asleep."

"But—"

"Babe, it's fine."

"I—" Words elude me. Did he say what I think he said? Did he just *Babe* me?

Silence. I turn back to the living room. There's no way Mark heard that. But the look on Mark's smug face makes me want to punch it.

Gilbert clears his throat. "Um, I was calling to see if you would let Royce in. He said he'd swing by this afternoon to run the final electrical inspection, so I can finally have the furnace and electricity through the house."

"Sure. Anything else?"

"Nah. We'll hang at the hotel until they get the interstate opened again. Looks like it'll snow throughout today. Should make it back tomorrow afternoon."

"Okay. Be safe."

"Sure thing."

I stare at Mark, who's staring at me with a dumb smile from the other room, and down half a cup of coffee. Mark doesn't have the chance to spill whatever he's thinking because a stampede of children attempting to be quiet boils over instead.

Diana enters with Lisa holding her hand. "Morning. Lisa says Mark's taking everyone for donuts. Hey, when did Jack wake up? And why is he chewing on—Mark, is that your key fob?"

"Yeah. He stole it from me."

"Alright. I'll have eggs and sausage ready when you get back." She finds a rubber giraffe under the coffee table and replaces the keys. "Cordy, you going with the gang?"

Mark heads to the kitchen, dodging around the kids, who dig through a mound of snow gear. "She is."

"I am?"

"Get your shoes on. I'll be ready in forty-five seconds."

Lauren sends me a look of panic then turns to her brother. "Hurry, Landon. Here's your other glove."

I tip back the rest of the coffee and stroll over to help. Kneeling on the carpet with the kids, I sort through the pile for Lisa's gloves and toss them to Diana. In thirty-eight seconds I've got gloves on all the kids. "Did everyone go pee? If you're ready, wait outside in the snow."

Diana disapproves of my announcement.

I speak loudly for everyone's benefit. "Better speak now or forever hold your pee."

She rolls her eyes.

"Why you so proper, sis? How would you say it?"

"It's just the way you yell it. 'Use the restroom,' would be better. Nevermind. You guys could take the van."

"And miss a blizzard walk?" I pull on my hat and look at her like she's lost her mind. "That's half the appeal of the donuts in the first place. It's our reward for conquering the blizzard." My fists plant on my hips in an instinctual Peter Pan pose.

Mark zips Nathan's coveralls over his pajama pants. "It's only twenty-seven degrees. We'll be fine. Help me with that baby wrap thing for Lisa."

Once we're all outside, bundled toes to nose, we start the exciting two blocks to the donut shop on the square. Lance and Leo are already wrestling in the yard.

Mark smiles with Lisa strapped to his back. I adjust the scarf over her face so only her cute little eyes with her blond lashes blink at me from her warm cocoon. "I love the desert, Cordy. But I forgot how much fun blizzard walks used to be." He glances at me with boyish humor in his eyes.

We step carefully onto the empty street. The only sounds are the kids running and laughing around us.

"I read all your texts." From the tone of Mark's voice, he's not even sorry. Just stating facts. "Forget everything I've said the past two weeks. That's who you need to go after." No one has ever accused Mark of beating around the bush. He's what you might describe as a felt-covered brick.

Generally, I like a friend who gets straight to the point. But I must disagree in this case. "I've never gone after a man. That's pathetic." The snow blows thick around us. The sun is muted and white. There is no sky. White, white, white everywhere.

"Why?" He turns to the side. "Come on, boys! Stay with us."

The twins launch to their feet and run with arms twirling until they're slipping and sliding beside us.

"Why?" Mark asks again.

"It's pretty obvious if he's not interested."

"And this Gilbert isn't interested?"

I quickly relate what I heard between him and John that

first day in Gilbert's house. "It would be relationship suicide. Gilbert made his position clear, and I would especially hurt John's feelings. I don't want to do that."

"You're not responsible for everyone's feelings."

"But shouldn't I attempt to give John a try? John's a really nice guy."

I'd like to think Mark's wincing at the snow and not at me. He shakes his head. "Do you ever listen to the stupid things you say? We're not syrups at a coffee shop or flavors at an ice cream parlor. You're not obligated to give anyone a try."

"John is really nice." There is no reason for me to defend John. Good golly. I'm so scared of believing Gilbert could ever choose me. Talking about it only makes it worse when it's so unattainable.

"You're being an idiot."

Now I'm mad. "You're a real friend, Mark. Super glad you're here." I move to the center of the street where it's not as slippery so I can angry-march without falling. "Why don't you just mind your own stinking business?"

"Why are you mad?" He tails me like sticky pizza dough I can't scrape off my hands. "Methinks the lady doth protest too much."

My cousin is infuriating! And this snow is not making me happy. There are no sweet fluffy flakes of artistic masterpieces. It's a blast of white stuff flying everywhere. My lips are so cold it's hard to talk. Whose idea was this anyway? Blizzard walks are stupid. The anger spikes. There's no call for it, but I feed it anyway. Heat vibrates through me, and sarcasm slides from my mouth. "It's swell hanging out with you. I always feel better about myself when you're around. A load of encouragement, that's you."

Lauren runs a few steps and tries to skate on the packed

snow of the tire tracks. The wind buffets against her and she falls flat. Laughing, she snags Landon's ankle and he pulls her a few feet until he falls on top of her. Lance and Leo scale the six-foot pile beside us that the snow plow left behind. I stop in the middle of the road and watch the kids frolic and squeal around us. Lisa smiles from her warm perch on Mark's back.

"Tell me you don't have feelings for Gilbert."

I don't honor him with a glance. "Next time you're paying full price for an Uber."

"Tell me you don't have feelings for Gilbert."

"Gag. *Feelings for.*" Face to the sky, the bits of ice melt on my skin. "I have feelings for you, Mark. Big ones. Big fat annoyed feelings. Don't talk to me about feelings. They're useless."

He swipes a leg under me, and I fall face first onto the ice, barely catching myself before I break my nose. "Ow! Geez Louise, Mark!"

He kneels beside me. "I'm sorry. I shouldn't have done that. I forgot we were on ice instead of snow. "

I rise to my hands and knees and hang my head between my arms as I catch my breath.

"Are you okay?"

"Just be grateful you have Lisa on your back or you'd be next."

"Fair enough."

I slowly climb to my feet and he gently takes my elbow. "Why did you do that? That was mean."

"I'm—I think I'm jealous."

"Of me?"

He nods. We walk in silence for a few steps while I mull that around. His grip tightens on my coat sleeve. "I've seen you struggle. I've seen you try so hard through the years to please everyone, and try to fit yourself into someone's idea of what you should be. Someone you're not. You'll never be loved for who you are if you're trying to be someone else. Sure, I haven't met this guy, but you could fill five notebooks with the conversations between the two of you. Trust me, no man talks to a girl that much if he's not into her."

I don't have much else to say. The kids run the last few yards and file into the donut shop ahead of us. If Mark is right, why am I so afraid?

29

CORDELIA

SUNDAY, DECEMBER 24

RYAN BAIRD/SOVEREIGN GRACE MUSIC—BEHOLD OUR GOD

B*ing!*

Mom: How's it going, sweety? Haven't heard from you in a few days.

Cordelia: Hi, Mom. I'm good. What's up?

Mom: Meet any nice boys from your app?

Cordelia: How's Diana?

Mom: If she didn't tell me I'd never know what's going on with you.

Cordelia: Working a lot. I finished the last Christmas cookbook!

Mom: Good job. Meet any nice boys from your app?

Cordelia: Had a nice dinner with David. But we won't meet again.

Mom: Oh, too bad.

Cordelia: No, it's good. We weren't a good fit.

Mom: When are you going to hang on to one of these men? I'm ready for more grandbabies.

I type out four different responses—none of them respectful or kind. The lights dim as church is about to start. Annoyed, I hold the power button on my phone until I can turn it off. Shouldn't have had the dumb thing out this morning anyway. I was hoping to hear from Gilbert, but he's still stuck in Omaha with the snow.

Diana nurses Jack beside me in the pew. His hand plays with a lock of her hair, and it's beautiful. She has six kids. Six kids and she's a mere two years older than me. That's wonderful for her, but Mom's words still bother me. She had no right to say it. No stinking right. Does Mom *think* before she opens her mouth?

"When are you going to hang on to one of these men? I'm ready for more grandbabies."

Oh, I don't know, Mom. When I'm all dried up and sour. I've looked hither and yon and nobody gets me. I'm pretty awesome by myself. Mostly.

There's always Facebook Marketplace. *ISO: A man to provide my mom with grandbabies. No holds. Bring your own truck.*

I know in my heart that she did not wake up today and ponder, "How can I make dear sweet Cordy miserable over the holidays?" But try telling that to whatever body part controls my emotions. Can we blame this on hormones? *Argh.* I'm furious—borderline livid. Why are people so dumb? A little voice in my head whispers oh-so-carefully,

Psst, you are also dumb sometimes. I grunt a small, reluctant noise in response that says, "I hear you, and I believe you, but my feelings are still bruised."

A short man with brown hair plays the simple, solemn opening chords on the grand piano. I breathe slowly and rest my mind.

"'Who created the heavens and stretched them out?'" I close my eyes and surrender my irritation, my unjustified anger, my worldly annoyance. My shoulders roll back and I join the song.

"'Who spread the earth from coast to coast?'" My God is so much more than I can comprehend. Not a being that has to count or measure. Those vast beaches were made *by* him and *for* him and *through* him. He doesn't count them because he *knows*.

"'Who gives breath to his people?'" A smile lifts my face. All creation praises our King.

Another musician with a striped green polo joins the piano with his guitar and this adds to the yearning tension in my soul as we begin the chorus. "'Who gives life to those who walk on it?'" Oh, God, I'm so, so unworthy, and yet I'm here worshiping. There is nowhere else I want to be. Standing in Your presence I am washed clean and made holy. "'Behold, the Creator! Behold the Lord. Sing His praise from the ends of the earth.'"

Drums come alongside the other instruments and they encourage this rising fullness in my heart as we start the second verse. "'Sing to the Lord a new song. Let the wilderness and cities raise their voices'"

Diana's alto harmony meshes beautifully with my soprano, and Lauren's young voice is on my other side. I take in the length of the pew where Landon and the twins sing too. The twins stomp out of rhythm and even though they are probably in competition to see who can stomp the fastest on the commercial grade carpet, they're here, and they're listening and learning. On the far end next to Landon, Mark stands with eyes closed, palms open. Lisa can't decide if she wants to face forward or backward as Nathan wrangles her on the other side of Diana. I can worship my God anywhere, but lifting my voice with my family is one of my greatest joys. Moving here was the right decision.

"'Let them give glory to the Lord.'" I can be such a fool. Such an impulsive, quick-acting fool. How many times has God reached down and saved me?

I lift on my toes. Compelled to *move*, I bounce as the music swells leading into the chorus again. Then I close my eyes and the words of the verse turn to pictures in my mind. "'The Lord will march out like a champion, like a warrior He will stir up His zeal. God forever. Jesus, Savior, risen to reign.'"

An ache in my throat blocks my words. Warmth washes over my arms, neck, and legs. I'm crying because my God is *good*. So, *so*, good. I'm crying because I'm overflowing with emotion that has to get out. There's angst and sorrow at what I've done and what Jesus did. There's overwhelming adoration too. The joy in my soul bubbles up and over and escapes as tears. It's lovely to be here, surrounded by the Lord's people.

"'He will turn darkness into light.'"

I picture God in this place. I imagine a throne at the head of our congregation. God the Father sits *right there* before us. Anyone walking in off the street might turn around and walk back out again because they don't see Him. They don't know Him. But if they would stay for a few minutes and hear this message. Behold! Look. At. Him.

Don't look at us and our faults and our failed attempts at being good on our own, but look at Him. We only want to point you to Him.

"'Let them give glory to the Lord.'"

His Spirit hovers around us and through us and in us. Jesus the Son... where is He? At first, I imagine Jesus on a throne too, but He won't stay there. He's standing in the pew next to me. He's walking around, shaking hands with His friends, and doing the bro shake with the hug and the slap on the back. He's embracing the elderly, kneeling before those that are too weak to stand, and high-fiving the preschoolers because He knows us intimately. We're His family. His brothers and sisters.

He comes and stands beside me and joins in our song. Jesus the Lamb and the Lion and the Heir sings to the Father.

I'm releasing these precious and wonderful tears of joy because He smiles at me, and I smile back because we're friends. Good, *good* friends. Good enough friends that He waves to his Dad and says, "She's with me," and it's my undoing. I don't even try to sing anymore as I swipe at the little rivers of salt water on my cheeks.

"'Let them give glory to the Lord.'"

Diana holds a flannel burp cloth covered with blue sail boats in front of my face, and I laugh as I take it to dry my eyes and blow my nose. She tilts her head and mouths, "I love you" and fresh tears join the party.

For once I don't resist my strong feelings. I sob into the cloth and welcome every last drop of love until I'm full to bursting. There's no room for doubt when you're filled up with the truth. With Diana's arm around me, I lean into her while Jack's squishy fist bonks against my face.

"I love you too, big sister."

30

CORDELIA

MONDAY, DECEMBER 25

MATT WERTZ—SNOW GLOBE

I'm slaving over a tray of cookies that I'm decorating on the counter before I join the rest of the crew for lunch when a knock at the cottage door interrupts. I glance at the clock on the microwave. It's not yet nine in the morning.

The knock comes again, and I drop the piping bag of blue icing. "Coming!"

I twist the lock and open the door to Gilbert grinning his face off, wearing his red-checkered flannel and swinging a metallic green gift bag.

"Hi!" I jump to him and he stumbles onto the snowy path. "You're back!" My pointed toes barely touch the ground while hanging from his neck. Gilbert's cheek is cold against mine when his arms come around me.

He shuffles us into the house, kicks the door shut and leans against it.

Embarrassed, I slide to the floor and tug at my green, Anne Shirley hoodie, gray leggings, and red fuzzy socks

224

with white snowflakes. This might be the same outfit I was wearing when we met.

"You've got a little—Here." He pulls his flannel over his wrist and wipes the side of my face. A streak of blue stains his sleeve. "I need your advice on something. Do you have a minute?"

"Sure, what's up?" I inspect my hands to make sure I'm not covered in any more icing. Ope, and I left some on the side of his head.

"Okay, so I'm noticing how much—" He cuts off when I run my fingers through his hair to comb out the blue sugar.

"Sorry. I accidentally got food in your hair."

"No worries. Can I use your printer?"

"Yeah, yeah. Of course." I speed walk to the bedroom and snatch the bra from the doorknob and shove it under my pillow. Hastily, I gather laundry from the floordrobe and toss it in the basket. Good enough. "Printer's ready." I press the power button on my machine and step away from my tiny desk.

"Thanks, I have it on here." He raises a purple thumb drive.

This bedroom shrinks to half its size in a matter of seconds. I'm thinking of our night together and how there's no way I'd have the same self-control to be this close to him overnight again. Gilbert takes up space like he belongs.

"I'll be in the kitchen." I walk backward. "Ok, see ya. Bye."

He starts to sit but stops. There's another bra on the chair. My blue one with the little pink flowers. Lord, take me now! "Gah, sorry." I swipe the offending article and throw it across the room then flee the premises before he has a chance to comment.

I need a cold drink. When did it get so hot in here? I

start to pull off my hoodie when I remember I'm not even wearing a bra! "Of course not," I mutter and shove my sleeves to my elbows instead. My kitchen is trashed. I stack my dirty dishes from the past couple days, wipe the table, sweep the floor, then get back to icing the snowflake cookies.

Three cookies later my mind is deep in its own world. Dreaming of what I could do instead of cookbooks. I haven't heard back from my agent about the Easter cookbook. If I don't sign for another full book, I'm not sure I can live on what I make with the pictures themselves. I'd love to write stories that matter. Interview Aunt Jewels. I'm sure she's got a lifetime of stories that need to be told.

Food and stories. Fories. Ha! No.

I pause too long and a blob of icing drips where I didn't mean for it to go. Set the cookie aside. Think. I chew the side of my lip and stare at the backsplash. Food blog. Great pictures. Recipes. It's been done a thousand times. How would mine be different? Stories. Food. Pictures. History.

What if I interviewed unique individuals—everyone's unique when you dig a little—core memories surrounding food... Recipes. Pictures. Core memories.

"I have a friend—" Gilbert's voice a few feet away intrudes on my thinking, and I fling the piping bag to the floor with a yelp.

"Don't sneak up on a person like that."

"I didn't sneak. I just came from—" He chuckles. "Your face lost its color. Sorry, I didn't mean to startle you."

"All good." I cross my arms and lean against the counter while trying not to ogle the gift bag at his feet.

He follows my gaze. "Wanna see what I got you first?"

I clap my hands and sit at the table with him. Inside the bag is a pair of bright red tennis shoes. "Oh. Very nice." I hold them up and admire the shiny leather. The rubber from the sole wraps around the heel of the shoe.

"Driving shoes." He sounds hesitant. "It's silly I guess. But these are better for driving. I thought—since you're still learning how to drive stick they'd be handy. Though with all this snow—"

"I love them. Thanks." I run to my room and come back with a pair of regular socks so I can try them on. Halfway back I spin and almost fall trying to return to my bedroom. On the dresser is the gift I bought for him. It's so lame I shouldn't even give it to him.

"Sorry, I didn't wrap it." I plunk the leather belt on the table once I make it back to the kitchen. "It's a belt. I saw it at the mall and thought of you. See, it's got the music notes engraved or whatever all over it. Since you play music and wear pants—"

"I love it. Thanks." His eyes dip in concentration.

Aw man, he hates it. A belt was a stupid thing to get. I shouldn't have bought him anything.

Gilbert offers that same smile that stole my breath in Aunt Jewels' entryway. "It's 'Für Elise.'"

"For who?"

He laughs. "Look." He points to a section and hums a familiar tune. "It's one of Beethovan's most popular compositions. 'Für Elise.' That's cool." Gilbert continues to hum while running his finger to the end of the leather as if he's reading. "Now! The real reason for my visit." He sets the belt gently to the side and places a manilla folder on the table.

"So serious." I straighten my posture. "I feel like I'm in trouble. Is this landlord business?"

He pops his lips with a shake of his head. "I have a friend who's interested in dating. He says he hasn't had any luck. Anywho. I mentioned the online thing like you're doing and he found a few prospects. I want you to give me your thoughts on these bios."

"Oooh. This is fun. I love this job! This is a great Christmas present. Snooping into your friend's love life." I rub my hands together. "Hit me. Wha'd'we got?"

His right cheek dimples in a half-grin. "Merry Christmas. I guess I'll take back the shoes. That'll save me a boatload." He grunts when I kick his shin with my new fancy shoes under the table. "So, I'm just going to read these first because I don't want you to judge the person by any obvious stereotypes or racial prejudices."

"I'm mildly offended." I give him the side-eye. "Are you implying my judgment is biased?"

He clears his throat. "Girl Number One. Quirky, fun, extremely sassy. I love parties and dancing. If there's music, I'm moving. I'm always up for a good time. The friend you call when you want to laugh and be cheered up."

I tap my lips in thought. "I don't hate her, but she could be a bit much. Next."

Gilbert orients the folder in such a way to hide the pages from me. "Girl Number Two. I'm a woman of my word and careful to follow through and meet deadlines. My friends are always asking me for favors because it's no trouble for me to stop and help someone else. I enjoy spending a quiet evening listening to music, cooking, and chatting with my best friends. I'm career driven—I want to offer my best work, but I'm careful not to let it overtake the rest of my life. Work supports life, not the other way around." He slaps the folder shut. "Thoughts?"

"Huh. Okay, okay. She's the exact opposite of the first girl. I like them both. She could be lame. For a first date, maybe Girl Number One? Who's your friend, though? Is it anyone I know? It's not John, is it?" I form my lips into a perfect O of surprise.

"There's more. Hang on."

"Right, but if I don't know who we're pairing these women with, it won't matter—"

"Give me your knee-jerk impressions first."

I wiggle in my seat and he flips to the next page. "How can I pick if—"

"Girl Number Three—"

"Can I take notes?"

"No."

"Can I see the pictures?" I inch my hand toward his papers. "I can't remember—" My hand suffers a swat. "Ow!"

"Not yet." His eyes snap and he gives me a reproving look, so I shut up. He is not going to budge on this.

"Geez. Fine. Do it your way."

"Girl Number Three—"

"But I think it's stupid."

He smushes his finger against my lips, and I blow a raspberry.

"Quiet. Girl Number Three. I'm a people person. I love to spend time with my besties, but I'm open to bringing new friends into my circle. When I walk into a room, I light up the whole place. People are drawn to me without knowing why. I wear my emotions like a graphic T-shirt so everyone knows that I'm genuine."

I shake my head in disgust. "This one is a hard no. Who sets up a dating profile like that? She really said besties? Gross." I straighten a pretend halo. "'I light up the room when I walk in.' Come on. You've got to show me this girl's picture. No way she's getting a date unless she's hot."

Gilbert sighs like he knew this was coming. He opens

the cream-colored folder and lays out six pages before me. They immediately remind me of a one-page sales flier. They're as unique as six different book genres. And yet...

They're all me.

All six of them. Six different pictures of me artistically themed with six different descriptions. "How did—" I blink, shocked. "Did you design these? These are amazing."

"Cameron helped. He's really good with computers. My idea was to stick your pictures in a row and write out the different bios."

"Cameron." Doesn't that beat all. "Cameron has skills. Gilbert, these are insanely good. Look at the coordinating font choices. The bold highlights along the side. The way he fits the picture into each page is unique and matches each theme. Holy moly." I gasp when I'm hit with an amazing idea. "Do you think he could help me design some of my own products? I have these really great recipes for cookbook pamphlets. I've never seen it done before. But imagine a week's worth of easy recipes that includes a grocery list. Breakfast, lunch, dinner. All in one small book. No fluff. But he could help put it all together and make it beautiful. They'd be outstanding. You know how many women want done-for-them meal plans? Diana and her friends would drool over something like this."

Gilbert's large hands cover the pages and block my view of the art. When I look at him his shoulders are shaking in silent laughter. He points to the bio of Girl Number Five. "Read this one."

I hold the paper up and read the words quietly. "I have amazing ideas. My secret power is thinking of ways to solve problems that nobody else has noticed. With the right team behind me, I'm unstoppable." My lips press together, and I take a jerky breath through my nose. It finally hits me what's going on here. Gilbert's saying really really nice things about me. "You really think so?"

Instead of answering he hands me another page. "Read this one."

"You read it." I whisper, afraid I'm going to embarrass myself with tears.

"Girl Number Six. I feel everything." Gilbert wraps my hand in his and keeps reading. "I love deeply. I'm passionate and excited to be alive. When I'm sad it consumes me, but when I'm joyful it fills the whole house. I smile and it feeds those around me."

"Oh, stop it." I try to take the paper from him, but he drops it and captures both of my hands.

"Cordelia, I lied. I don't have a friend looking for a girl-friend. It's me."

I grip his calloused fingers tightly, afraid this isn't real. "But these descriptions aren't me, they aren't—"

"They're all you. They're what I see when I look at you. I'm not choosing just one part. I want all sides of you."

I stare back in disbelief. Gilbert's delusional. He doesn't know what he's saying.

"Even now, you're shaking your head like you don't believe me. Cordelia, you're not just this or just that. You're all of this and so much more." He pushes the pages closer to me. "And so am I. I'm not a musician or a handy-man. I'm not a nephew or a son or a brother. I'm all of it."

"But you—what happened to you not dating?"

The smile that he shoots toward me is my kryptonite. "Someone told me I was being an idiot." He disengages one of his hands and gently cups the side of my face. "My idea of dating didn't match our friendship. When we're together I'm not worried about the money or the time, I just like being with you. I don't have much, and I'm really busy, but if we keep going the way we've started, I can't stay just your friend. I want more."

An anxious laugh spills from me. I'm nervous and excited. Gilbert is saying the sweetest things, and I don't want to mess it up. I've never seen him so serious. Even when he sliced his arm and I had to drive him to the clinic, he laced everything with humor.

He pushes the pages away from us. "I was afraid to show you these because I don't want to put you in a few boxes. You're so much more than these six pages, and I want to learn everything about you." He stands from his chair and tugs me up in front of him. "Will you choose me?"

"Yes," I breathe out the word and then find my voice. "Oh my goodness, yes."

He smiles while swinging our hands between us. The moment stretches into silence.

"So..." No worries, you can always count on me to fill it. "What happens now?"

A faint flush creeps along his neck. "Can I kiss you?"

I laugh because I'm so happy, but my laugh turns into a giggle and I cover my mouth because I'm so embarrassed.

Gilbert slides his hands to my shoulders and pulls me against him while I recover from this overflow of happiness. His embrace is everything, and I could live here. He kisses the top of my head and it lights me on fire. "I love your zest for life. Don't dim that down, ever."

As long as he sticks around, I have the feeling I won't need to. I'm just about to work up the courage to kiss him, when my kitchen door flies open. I swallow a scream and pull away from Gilbert on instinct.

He holds me tight instead and turns us both to face the door.

Cameron stands there triumphantly. "Ah-ha! I knew it would work. I'm a marketing genius."

Gilbert grumbles, and I feel it deep in his chest against my ear. "Not now, Cameron. I'm a little busy."

"I see that. Dad's on the computer back at the house. He's only got a minute. Come say hi right quick and you can get back to your canoodling."

Cameron slams the door and Gilbert softens against me. "I should probably mention I invited Cam to live with me until he finds another job. Or forever. I don't know."

"Merry Christmas, Gilbert." My eyes fill up with happy tears and I don't even try to wipe them away.

"Merry—"

Cam returns with a rush of winter air. "No more of this. Come on."

"I'm coming!" Gilbert takes my hand and drags me along. I guess we're both going.

Squinting at the blowing snow across my yard while warm and joy-filled tears freeze on my snotty face isn't how I pictured Christmas Day going.

Let it be known that strong women cry. Sometimes a lot. But only because we're not afraid to be ourselves with the people who love us.

CORDELIA

TEN MONTHS LATER

"That's quite the list, Cordy. Let's see if we can't pare it down a little."

"Hardly! It's all important." I shake the notebook in front of the laptop camera.

"Very much so. Your life is full to the brim. Obviously, you've had a great week. But I need you to remember, the higher your highs—"

"The lower my lows. Yes, so you've said, yet when I'm feeling this way it doesn't make any logical sense to stop it. If the train's on the right track, why slow it down?"

My counselor shakes her head with a huge smile on her face. "Because trains running at that speed are doomed to crash or run out of coal. Use up all the coal, and you'll have a hard time getting up the next hill."

She's probably right. I love her to pieces, but I've got a lot of fight left in me today. "The track is clear! Straight ahead. Choo-choo! Samantha, Samantha. Listen. I'll just get through this next week and then I'll rest."

Samantha yanks a rubber band from her wrist and flings it toward me. It flies somewhere behind her camera. "No.

That's who you were before you hired me. That's the kind of thinking that lands you in bed when you don't want to be there. You have to make time to rest, or your body will rest all on its own. It won't pick a convenient time for you. Go through that list again. Let me hear it."

I raise my day book and clear my throat. "A thousand words on Royce's fried apples by Monday. Bake cookies with Lisa. Call the guests who didn't RSVP for Mark's engagement party. Schedule two more reels for Hadley Strings and draft the newsletter. Go through the photos from last night's gig and edit five for a post. Send the final tour schedule to the printer. Finish packing for the weekend—"

"Ah, that one. Do that one first."

"But Gil and I don't leave until tomorrow afternoon."

"Are you paying me to help you, or do you like throwing your money away?"

"Lands to the living, Samantha, you're a tyrant. Fine."

"You've got this. I'd love to keep talking, but it's about time to sign off. Chin up. If you get overwhelmed next week, stop and name the emotion. 'I'm feeling XYZ because ABC.' And it's okay to feel what you're feeling. Listen to what that emotion is trying to tell you, but you mustn't stay there. Then you're going to speak out loud and write down the truth. 'The truth is I am capable of this task because I've done it before, because I can ask for help, because I can learn new things, because I'm a woman of my word...' Look at the facts of the matter, name the truth, and then back it up with evidence. The whole truth is that Cordelia Jane Conner is chosen by God. She has direct access—"

I whisper with Samantha the truth she speaks over me every week. "I have direct access to the Creator of the universe. I am holy, set apart, and beloved. I am the Lord's."

"Amen." Gilbert's warm voice alerts me to his presence before his arms circle me in my desk chair. "Hi, Samantha. Anything I need to know?"

"Hello, Gilbert. She needs a body double until she's packed for the weekend. She's going to do that right now."

"Got it." He squeezes me once and kisses my temple. "I'll grab us a packing snack."

Samantha waves through the laptop screen. "Bye for now."

I stare at my list of to-dos and feel the stress building against the onslaught of responsibility. Breathe. Breathe, breathe, breathe. It's fine. I got this. Under the last item I scribble another bullet point with my new favorite sentence.

Cordelia Conner is chosen.

I smile. The words are like a high five, fist pump, and victory dance smashed into a motivational sandwich.

"Babe!" Gilbert calls from our downstairs kitchen in the big house. "Cam just called. I invited him for dinner."

I chuckle. Of course he did. As soon as we were married, we let Cameron have the cottage. Turns out Cam is an extremely talented graphic designer, and John and I put him to work creating graphics for the band.

John's—well, *our*—website sells merchandise now. Shirts, hoodies, hats, stickers. We have digital tracks for sale with folk songs and contemporary hits, and the boys are wrapping up a new Christmas album for the next season. The secret sauce that first got us rolling? Nursing homes. Yep. I stepped in as manager an hour after our first kiss and booked Hadley Strings at over a hundred nursing homes by the end of February.

With my endless supply of ideas, John's ability to get things done, Cameron's graphics for marketing and merchandise, Gilbert's musical genius—and dashing smile—

the band brings in more than enough money for the four of us to live comfortably without ever leaving Nebraska.

I didn't sign another cookbook deal with a publisher. John quit his job. Gilbert paid off his construction loan. Cameron now has three bosses who won't let him quit. Mark's getting married to—well, that's another story.

And me?

I'm still writing—but only for myself. I started a simple food blog gathering recipes from around town, and it grew into this magical place for people to share core memories involving food. This weekend, Gilbert and I are traveling west to interview a ninety-seven-year-old rancher in the sandhills, who started as the cook's gopher when he was six. He's been bringing food out to cowboys every day since. There's a warm ball of excitement and purpose surrounding this weekend. I can feel it in my bones that it's where I'm supposed to be.

Gilbert peeks into the office, his eyebrows lowered in concern. "You good? I got nachos in the bedroom. Aren't we supposed to be packing?"

"Yeah, just help me out of this chair. I think I'm stuck." Not stuck. But I'll take any chance for him to hold me and he knows it.

"Oh, I'll help you all right." My husband, the dear that he is, scoops me from the chair, saunters down the hall and dumps me onto the rug at the foot of our bed. "I waited thirty years for a wife to cook and clean for me. And look what happened?" He gestures to our bed piled with two loads of clean laundry, three note-books, and my purse's entire contents scattered along the side because I'd lost my favorite pen.

"Hmm." I climb to my feet and survey the damage. "There appears to have been a struggle."

"Indeed." He points to the mess. "You'll put the laundry away or no nachos for you."

"Gasp!"

Cracks form in his facade of irritation. "You're not supposed to say 'gasp.' You just—gasp." Gilbert demonstrates how to gasp, and I mimic him like the perfect wife that I am. "No, higher, like this." This time he brackets his face with jazz hands. Oh, the drama.

I shrug. "I dunno. I think I'd rather kiss for a while and not do the laundry."

He tries to play it cool but quickly fails. With the tip of his tongue caught between his teeth, he dances closer to me.

I slide my palms up his gray T-shirt and link my fingers behind his neck. "I'm so glad you chose me."

He kisses my nose. "Ditto."

"I waited a long time for you."

"Sure, you did." He pulls me flush against him. "How long were we friends before you made your move? Two days? Taunting me with desserts I'd never even heard of before?"

"You're the one who injured yourself in an attempt to meet the girl next door. And then all that snow! Shoveling right outside my window. How could I possibly resist?" I kiss him. His cheeks are smooth with a fresh shave and he smells like soap.

He speaks with his eyes closed. "Next time will you at least let me propose first?"

"Next time don't wait around so long after I find a ring in your wallet."

"Stay out of my wallet."

"Shh. I'm trying to kiss my husband." My phone buzzes in my back pocket and Gilbert slips it out and turns it off before I even get to see who's calling. "Hey! That could be important."

"Nope. Samantha said you're supposed to pack. No distractions." Says the man pressing his lips under the side of my jaw.

Instead of swooning at his romance, I giggle. I'm the happiest girl in the whole wide world. If he wasn't holding me here, I'd probably be flying.

"What're you giggling for, wife?"

"I was just thinking of my friend Anne. You know what she would say here?"

"Tell me."

"'Dear old world, you are very lovely, and I am glad to be alive in you.'"

"And what would Anne's Gilbert say?"

I think for only a moment before the words come to me, "He says, 'We are going to be the best of friends. We were born to be good friends, Anne.' Except you can put in my name instead."

He smiles jubilantly, as I always imagined my someday Gilbert would. "We were born to be good friends, Cordelia."

And the way he speaks the truth encompasses everything I love about this man. I've made a thousand mistakes in my short life, but waiting for Gilbert will never be one of them.

ACKNOWLEDGMENTS

Dedicated to the Author and Perfecter of my faith;
it is only by His mercies that we are not consumed.

"But you are a chosen people, a royal priesthood, a
holy nation, God's special possession, that you may
declare the praises of him who called you out of
darkness into his wonderful light."
   —1 Peter 2:9 NIV

This story came about when I had it settled in my mind to
write a short, fun, contemporary novel that I would give
away to entice newsletter subscribers. I was going for
10,000 words. Ehh, okay how about 30,000. Well, if you're
going to go through all the trouble of creating well-rounded
characters, you can hardly tell their story with less that
50,000. Ahahaha. The final count is 59,780 words (not
including this piece that I'm writing the night before I order
print copies without even paying an editor to look through it
first. What kind of crazy author am I?)

The point is that once Cordelia introduced herself to
me, she had way too many things to say for a novella.

Waiting for Gilbert is a love letter to myself. I cried
through chapter two when Aunt Jewels arrived. (By the
way, I didn't write her character, she wrote herself.) And
then chapter 29 happened. I could hardly type for the tears

washing my face. I wrote the church scene very early in the process.

When I started, I wasn't sure if I was going to write a "Christian" romance, or just a nice romance with Christian characters. After Jesus walked all over chapter 29, he made his point pretty clear.

A few more neat facts you might find interesting:

My friend Heather is delightful. Everyone should get themselves a bosom friend. She doesn't know this book is for her. (Except she probably does now. Hi, Heather! Can I tell them about the one time I shared about how I'd hired an accountability coach to help me with life and you said, "That's exactly what everyone with ADHD needs!" And it was awkward because you'd just accidentally diagnosed me because you thought I already knew—and then I answered, "Wait, do you mean me? Or... people... in general. You meant me?!" Turns out you could spot it two miles away. I did start meeting with a counselor, and I will forever be grateful to learn there's nothing wrong with me, and I'm not crazy, and sometimes I just need to wear earplugs and cry, and makes lists upon lists that include "eat food."

Pretty much everything sweet in Gilbert is actually Heather... so. Do with that what you will.

Michelle, I didn't know this book was for you until I'd finished. I realized how much Cordelia relies on Diana without consciously knowing it. Big sisters are like that. They love their little sisters even with no rewards. They love their little sisters even when little sisters are a bit eccentric. So, thanks.

Dad, you'll probably never read this, and that's okay. But I feel like I need to acknowledge your influence on my life. You showed me and my sisters how to do hard things. How to read directions and think. I've lived in the shell of a house while you taught us how to hang drywall. We've lived in the crumbling beast of a cottage. Writing a book is kind of like building a house, and I'm grateful you taught me how.

Mom, Robin, Reuben, Kylie, Jaci, and JoAnn—I love you. Thanks for your continual encouragement and excitement for my stories.

Megan Schaulis, I'm so happy we found each other. What are the chances we'd join scribes at the same time and submit chapters the same week? God-given friends are truly wonderful. Thanks for your friendship and of course your extremely valuable editorial insights. Many of your words blended into this book to make it beautiful.

Christine, Mevia, Jennifer, Nix and so many more Bookstagram friends who believed in this story before it was finished. Thank you.

Ben, dearest husband, do you remember the first time you called me Babe? Yeah, I don't either, it's been a few years. I've officially been dating you for more than half of my life. You're the best. Thanks for letting Gilbert borrow your work clothes. I wouldn't have dressed him in anything else.

Dear readers, if you loved this story, be sure to tell your friends. :-) Word of mouth is the absolute best way to share good news. If this story just wasn't your type, that's okay too. You might prefer my historical fiction instead, *Bluebird on the Prairie* and *Wildflower on the Prairie* are both set in 1879 Nebraska, seven miles from Hadley Springs.

Alas, I've gone on long enough. I really should get to work on Mark's happily ever after now.

LET'S CHAT!

I look forward to hearing from you. Join my newsletter and get Cordelia's eggnog cream pie recipe! Maybe someday I'll write that bonus scene my editor recommended about Gilbert and Cameron creating Cordelia's biography pages, and I'll send it to you... But first I need to eat lunch.

Companion material includes *Cordelia's Day Book*. A planner with everything simple and straightforward to keep you on schedule. It's a chore list, calendar, notebook, and budget keeper all in one. Find it online.

www.TashaHackett.com

ALSO BY TASHA HACKETT

- *Bluebird on the Prairie*
- *Wildflower on the Prairie*
- *Kindergarten Math: Teach Me to Number My Days*

Bluebird on the Prairie: Hearts of the Midwest, Book 1: In the 1879 prairie town of Ockelbo, Nebraska, Eloise keeps house for her brother and cares for her toddler nephew, Luke. She exists to be useful to those two and nothing else. She hides from the world— lost in grief for her husband who tragically died their first year of marriage.

Zeke is only passing through on his way to California until he falls headfirst into a creek where Eloise is playing with little Luke in nothing but her unmentionables. *Gasp*

Wildflower on the Prairie: Hearts of the Midwest, Book 2: Hannah Benton is determined to escape the confines of her critical and controlling mother. The best way to obtain freedom is to get married! She has three months to find a husband... she can do it, but it sure doesn't leave time to dilly-dally.

Kindergarten Math: Teach Me to Number My Days: This 100 lesson course is designed specifically for the Christian homeschool family. It makes use of the Bible, a calendar, pencil and paper, counting bears, and pattern blocks, but there are no worksheets. It's a beautiful student-teacher conversation to look forward to each day.

Made in the USA
Monee, IL
23 October 2024